Bernard Greenwood

The Dealings of God with a Laborer

Or, the experience of Bernard Greenwood

Bernard Greenwood

The Dealings of God with a Laborer
Or, the experience of Bernard Greenwood

ISBN/EAN: 9783337250324

Printed in Europe, USA, Canada, Australia, Japan

Cover: Foto ©Andreas Hilbeck / pixelio.de

More available books at **www.hansebooks.com**

OF

GOD WITH A LABORER;

OR,

THE EXPERIENCE

OF

BERNARD GREENWOOD.

WRITTEN BY HIMSELF.

IN THREE PARTS:

PART   I.   MY EXPERIENCE IN GERMANY.
PART II.   MY EXPERIENCE IN AMERICA.
PART III.   MY EXPERIENCE IN THE MINISTRY.

RALEIGH, N. C.:

EDWARDS, BROUGHTON & CO., STEAM POWER PRINTERS AND BINDERS,
1884.

INTRODUCTION.

I am a native of Germany, born in Weener, East Friesland, Kingdom of Hanover, on the 24th of September, 1827. There also I united with the church of God (a Free Grace Baptist church) in August, 1853, and emigrated to this country in May or June, 1854. After seven weeks sailing on the Atlantic ocean, we landed at New York, in August same year. One week's stay at that city was for me full of experience of the goodness of our God and of His care toward me in providence and grace.

We went to Cincinnati, Ohio, and dwelt there about five months. I was in the meantime trying to find Free Grace Baptists there, but with no success. Then my lot was cast at Clover, Clermont county, Ohio, where I resided till 1858, and, after a search of two years and a half, I was successful in finding the Old School or Primitive Baptists. I joined the Clover church by experience, though I could then tell only an outline, if I may so speak, of what I

knew the Lord had done for me. But they received me with gladness of heart and gave me liberty to try to tell in public what I had told them
in private. Since then I have been trying, with the
ability that God giveth, to set forth the crucified
Jesus, to proclaim the finished work of Christ. To
speak of His resurrection and ascension. To feast
on the electing love of God in Christ Jesus. Of the
regenerating power of the Holy Ghost and of his
goings forth conquering and to conquer, until the
hard heart of the sinner be broken, and all the redeemed are brought home to be saved to sin no
more.

Thus from Clover I moved a licensed preacher to
Lynchburg, Ohio. Now for the first time I began
to write out a little of my experience, and it was
published in the *Signs of the Times* in (I think) 1859.
In 1869 and 1870 I sent it written more fully to
Elder E. H. Burnam, editor of the *Regular Baptist
Magazine.*

In 1860 I moved to Charleston, W. Va., where I
also found brethren and a church a few miles from
that place. There were some beloved colored brethren in the town of Charleston. They wished me to
break the bread of life to them in that town, and

bringing my case before the church at Lynchburg the brethren there agreed to ordain me to the work of the ministry on the 23d of March, 1861. Thus I was sent forth of the brethren, who commended me to the grace of God.

In 1862 I moved from Charleston to Hillsboro, Ohio, where I stayed till 1865. My membership was then at Brush Creek church, Highland county, Ohio. Thence I moved to Madison, Ind., where I found no Baptists.

In 1866 I moved to Evansville, Ind., where I found a church. I lived in that place till 1869, gave in my letter from Brush Creek church and enjoyed myself exceedingly in fellowship with the English brethren. And there I found also two German believers who could talk no English. My stay was not yet. So far there had been no certain dwelling place for me. I moved from Evansville, the beloved place, where also my soul has suffered much, and went to Corydon, Ind. There I gave in by experience and was received, preaching to the loved ones till 1871. Thence I moved to Columbus, Ind. Over eight years I lived there in worldly prosperity, but was destitute of the society of God's dear people.

There were only a few scattered believers in that part of Indiana.

Now a great desire came over me to live at some place where believing Baptists held their meetings every Sunday. For two whole years I was trying to escape my loneliness. With sighs and groans, and supplications, with longing desires and tears, I have made known my petitions to God, and the Lord hearkened and heard the groanings of his poor prisoner. He graciously granted me my request and directed me to Wilson, N. C., where I have resided since January, 1880. Thus, while I once more begin to write "my experience," I am mindful of this fact, that the dear Lord has been gracious to me all the days of my life. Oh, my soul, bow at his footstool low, for he had compassion on his poor worm. He brought his wandering sheep to his dear fold again. The Lord caused me to find favor among his dear children here, for they have received me as one of the family. They loved to hear me tell of the wondrous works of Jehovah Jesus, and they glorified God concerning me.

PART I.

MY EXPERIENCE IN GERMANY.

CHAPTER I.

BELOVED READER :

In giving my experience to the Church, I shall begin at the beginning, with the heart-sickening truth that the first sixteen years of my natural life I have lived without hope and without God in the world. I was dead in sin, and knew not God. The follies of youth took a strong hold on me. I loved darkness rather than light, cursing and swearing and smutty tales and anecdotes came as natural to me as was possible. I was Satan's captive, who had power to mould me at his will, but God, who is rich in mercy, did not leave my soul in prison, nor leave me in the filth of sin. I was not to perish with the world, blessed be his holy name for ever and ever. Amen.

Impressions of eternity, or so-called religious impressions, I have had sometimes, but they would all wear off and soon be forgotten, for the thought of eternity made me afraid and became awful to my mind. My parents were no professors of religion, but they trained me up from early childhood to read in the Bible aloud to them. I was brought up in the Reformed Church, a born Gentile, and not a Jew even outwardly.

The nearest the Reformed Church comes to any in this country, is the Presbyterian.

Early in life I got my head stuffed full of notions as to a do and live system of religion, and believed what some had told me—that I was about as good a christian as ever I need be; was sprinkled in in-fancy and confirmed when fourteen years of age, I was considered as a full member, who had a right to their communion table. About this time I was put to the tailor's trade in my father's workshop, and for two hours a day, (Saturday and Sunday ex-cepted,) for two years my parents sent me to a high school to study the higher branches of German grammar. Reading aloud in the shop was also kept up. It was novel reading, however, and only some-times in the Bible. This novel reading took a de-cided hold on my mind, and tended to excite me to such a degree, that in the day I would think about them and dream of them in the night; they seemed to become a second part of my life, like the food was to the body. The Bible became now a dry and un-interesting book to me. I thought to become like one of those heroes in novels was far preferable to all religion, because they were worthies, they always carried their point, because they were so noble and true; or like one in love-stories, who was a devoted slave to his fair one, and after much opposition won her by his honesty of purpose. Though poor for a long while, yet in the end he was successful, bearing off the palm through his persistent efforts of fair dealing, good morals, and true manliness of character. Such things I coveted after, and the like I would declaim in company of my young friends.

When I at one time was reading a poem called *The Minstrel's Curse* (Des Seanger's Fluch), which I knew by heart, quite unexpected my father came into the room. I kept on, however. He heard me patiently, and when I got through I thought he might chide me for the foolishness, but instead, he said: " Well done," and said that he regretted that he was not able to send me to the University and have me educated as a preacher." So, because my parents had not the means, I was not so educated.

I learned my trade, but all this time I knew not God. I can but review the years of childhood and youth in silent awe and wonder. While I write this, I am astonished at the long-suffering of a covenant-keeping God. With thanksgiving and praise, I would sing his loving kindness in the night, and his keeping care over a worthless worm like me, even when dead in sin! Oh, my soul, praise him! He spared not the angels that sinned, but cast them

down to hell, whilst I was born in sin and loved
sin—I, a child of wrath, was spared and not cut off!
Who spared not the old world, though they were
not worse than others, but spared me, who was
equally as bad as they.

Wonder, O heavens, and be astonished, O earth !
Who turned the cities of Sodom and Gomorrah into
ashes, condemning them with an overthrow, but I—
let me speak it with reverence—I am here to-day, a
spared monument of the grace of God ! " What shall
I render unto the Lord for all his benefits toward
me ?" O God, I will render praises unto thee ! Many
who were much better than I have been called away
in their youth—death has gathered them to the dust
again ; many have died as they lived, without leav-
behind them any evidence of their acceptance with
God, while I have been spared to behold the salvation of the God of Israel !

> Pause, my soul, adore and wonder :
> Say, O why such love to me?

The days of my youth have I spent in folly, and
the years as a tale that is told, yet have I been kept
just outside of a gaping hell, to see the justice of
God in all things, and to learn

> That if my soul were sent to hell,
> Thy righteous law approves it well.

When in the days of youth I neither hoped for
heaven nor cared for hell, even then God cared for

me and kept me from perishing, until he would quicken me into life, and bring me to Jesus Christ, his beloved Son, to whom be honor and power everlasting. Bless the Lord, O my soul, and all that is within me bless his holy name. He hath not dealt so with any other nation, and as for his judgments, they have not known them. All ye that wait for the salvation of God, praise ye the Lord.

CHAPTER · II.

Never shall I forget the consternation I felt when I was awakened at the hour of midnight with the words, "God is holy, what art thou?" Although the words do not stand in canonical order in the Bible, nevertheless they came to me as the word of the Lord. For the first time in my life I saw myself a miserable, hell-deserving sinner. I cannot describe the feelings I had at the awakening. A holy God! a condemned sinner! What awful disparity! I wept aloud, and my brother, who was in bed with me, heard and asked if I was sick? I said, "No, John, I am such an awful sinner." He paid no further attention to it or me, and slept on. But I could not sleep any more that night. I was determined to say no more about it to any one. I felt that no one in this world could help me, and to God the

Holy One I could never come. My sins now came all up before me: like Pharoah's host they were after me, like swarms of locusts they arose, and darkness and death eternal stared me in the face. Oh! the horror of that night. Early in the morning I got up and sought and found the Bible. I took the Book to a place where I might be by myself, but not a word could I find to suit my case. My fellow workmen in the shops did not know what to make of my appearance and conduct. They noticed a change, but attributed it to sickness. I could not eat. I wept more than anything else. The tears would come. I strove to keep them back, but could not. This lasted for several days. One morning early I arose and opened the Bible once more, and where it fell open I read: "Arise, shine, for thy light is come, and the glory of the Lord is risen upon thee." Isaiah 60: 1. This completely overcame me. I could read no further. I closed the Book. With it came a rejoicing in my sin-smitten soul, which seemed to lift me above earth, above sin, above all my misery, mourning, lamentation and woe. The words were Gospel, the tidings of salvation to me. The workmen in the shop told me I looked like one who had suddenly fallen heir to some large estate. And so I had. I could not explain. It had come so sudden. I could not utter my happiness. For some time I lived as though I had never sinned.

The multitude of my sins were all driven back, and I felt peace and happiness reign in my heart.

But a change took place. In an answer to one of the men, I used the name of God in vain! Immediately I felt guilty again. I ran out of the shop— weeping took the place of rejoicing. I was much distressed. I hunted for the same text again which had brought such uninterrupted joy for a season. I found it, but lo, the power and sweetness of it was gone! and I remembered that I had read it many times before, and wondered how it could have given me such great joy only lately. Now my eyes fell on the next verse: "For behold the darkness shall cover the earth, and gross darkness the people." Isaiah 60: 2. This I concluded was my case; I was of the earth, and darkness had come upon me, according to the word of the Lord!

And if I did not belong to the people spoken of there, gross darkness must be my portion too, for the mouth of the Lord hath spoken it. Now, I said to myself, I am determined to break myself from all my bad habits, I will entirely quit swearing at any cost. I formed resolutions and would act upon them; I would become religious, and then go to the communion table. For a time I was on my guard, I did not want to think even a wrong thought, but wrong and sinful thoughts would come unsought, unasked, and ere I was aware I beheld and was assured that my heart was full of them. This worried me greatly. To the world I tried to go and mingle again with my former companions, but lo! the pleasures of the world were turned into plagues to me, and my friends would call me, mockingly, the quaker or the preacher. Why not altogether join the church and become one of God's people? But then I felt my unworthiness, and to God's people such a horrid sinner as I could never belong. Sometimes the horror of great darkness was so thick upon me that I would arise in the night and go quickly to some field and kneel down or fall on my face trying to pray. But when I got there I could not pray. I thought I must keep trying, and trying again to break myself from sinning. The Lord would not hear me as long as I was committing sin. Sometimes I would go to a night-prayer meeting. A few god-fearing people would meet, and I got to hear of it. I went and heard them read, talk and pray, and sing, and for a little while I imagined I felt better. But, oh, my foolish heart! I still lived the old ways of boyish follies, and got into them again in earnest. Now I resolved to give up all religious notions, and keep on with the world as best I could. I could not bear the thought of acting the hypocrite, and the way I was going on was nothing but hypocrisy. To visit prayer-meetings and trying to associate with godly people—and then still lust after the follies of youth, was inconsistent. Either religion must go or the world. Of this I felt more and more assured. I thought may be I might easily lay religion aside forever, and if I was to show by my conduct that I was no religionist, but was just like the rest of boys, they would then quit teasing me and holding me up as some pious youth. But I was mistaken. I could not forget the words that first had come to me at midnight: "God is holy." They followed me wherever I went. And I kept on resolving to do better, yet every time, as opportunity afforded, I would be found engaged in some foolishness again. So time passed, and I saw myself, instead of getting better, grow worse and worse. Now the conviction came to me that I had justly deserved eternal death. That it was beyond my reach to obtain forgiveness of sins. I could do nothing to get into favor with God, who is the holy God. I cried, but there was no answer! I prayed, but God did not hear me. What to do I knew not. I was like one desperate. Nothing but sin could I call my own. What must I do to be freed from sin? What must I do to be saved? No relief, no help appeared. In my anguish and bitterness of soul I concluded and cried, I am lost—lost to all eternity!

CHAPTER III.

About this time I left home with a firm resolve
to do better.   And if I could find out what my duties were, I would do them; and thus, as I was
taught, obtain peace and forgiveness.   And by duties (works) I would atone for all my former conduct.   Moreover, I resolved to become good, and do
good, and cease to do evil, and then God would have
mercy on me; and, as it is the whole duty of man
to fear God and keep his commandments, I would
begin at once, and begin in earnest.   I went to the
city of Emden, and got work in a tailor shop, but
failed to work with a will as I had resolved to do
I felt a spell of sickness come over me.   When by·
myself, I could do nothing but weep, and when in
the shop I trembled and sighed.   The proprietor
soon found out he could do nothing with me, and
then sent me away sick and penniless.   I more staggered than walked out of town.   I felt I had to give
up.   Vengeance had overtaken me, and I felt as
though I was about to be dragged into hell.   I wished
for some place where no mortal could see me, and
then I could die there and await and receive my
doom.   Condemned, justly condemned, I felt I could
no longer live.   I wished for rocks and mountains
to fall on me, and hide me from the face of him that
sitteth on the throne, and from the wrath of the

Lamb.   At last I found such a place in a large open field.   I almost crawled to the spot.   I was sure no mortal eye could see me, nor mortal ear hear my groanings.   I prayed to the devil to deal mercifully with me when he had me finally in hell, as I thought I had not been so very much overwicked after all. I sank down on the grass, as one dead.   I expected to awake amidst the flames of hell.   My sins had crushed me down, and I thought were dragging me to endless perdition.   Then I became unconscious, and knew no more.   While in this state of unconsciousness, I saw all my sins exposed in a crucified person, who appeared to me as the crucified Saviour. I knew it was Jesus, but looked with astonishment at my sins being exposed in Christ.   While I was gazing with speechless wonder, a voice proceeded from the crucified Saviour, and he spoke to me in the German tongue: "Come unto me, thou weary and heavy laden, and I will give thee rest."   I answered, and cried: What! Me, O Lord?   I am such an awful sinner!   And the crucified Saviour answered, and said : I, even I, have blotted out all thy transgressions for my name's sake, and thy sins and thy iniquities will I remember no more!   My soul was filled with speechless awe, I trembled with fullness of joy.   When I found utterance, I said : I have heard of thee by the hearing of the ear, but now mine eye seeth thee; wherefore, O Lord, I abhor myself, and repent in dust and ashes.   Then, at once

consciousness returned. I found myself lying on my
face; I sprang to my feet, looked around, and said
to myself, what was this? I felt and pinched my
arm to be assured that it was my body still on earth;
everything looking brighter, everything seemed to
look glorious all around. I said, where are my sins?
where is my misery? where my sickness? where
was that awful burden of guilt? They were no
more pressing me down. They were gone—all gone.
I felt as light as air, I thought; and to assure myself, I danced around, I sprang up in the air, I ran,
then fell on the ground, then got up again, leaping
and praising God. Adoration, thanksgiving and
praise flowed like living water from my lips; I wept
tears of joy and gratitude; my heart and soul were
full of praise. Oh! the rapturous thought, Jesus
loved me! Jesus called me, and assured me of the
full and free forgiveness of all my sins. Yea, beloved reader, I was so overcome that I stood still
awhile, took off my hat, viewed the spot, and then
said: Here is God. Mine eyes have seen the Lord
of hosts. Praise his name, O my soul! Sing praises
to Jehovah Jesus; sing praises to the mighty God!
He hath removed all my sins from me: he will remember them against me no more forever. Oh!
blessed day! Oh! glorious hour! Then, in rapturous song I cried with tears of joy: Bless the Lord, O
my soul, and all that is within me bless his holy
name! Bless the Lord, O my soul, and forget not

all his benefits! who forgiveth all thine iniquities, who healeth all thy diseases, who redeemeth thy life from destruction, who crowneth thee with loving-kindness and tender mercies. Ps. 103: 1, 4. When my sins had arisen against me mountain high, the mighty God overthrew these mountains—I am saved!—saved from hell's destructive power, saved from death, from sin and sin's exceeding sinfulness. I am a new creature, and even my bodily sickness was cured by the Heavenly Physician then and there. After a little time of thus feasting after long fasting, I went my way rejoicing, never more to behold with my bodily eyes the spot where I had obtained the blessing of my beloved Saviour, God—blessings eternal, even life evermore. Therefore will I give thanks ūnto thee, O Lord, among the heathen, and sing praises unto thy name. Ps. 18: 49.

CHAPTER IV.

I went to Aurich and found work immediately. The man said, boy as I was, he would give me a trial. I worked a week for him and with him, when a feeling came over me which I could not resist. I wanted to go home. The proprietor of the shop however protested. He said—was there anything amiss on his part? I told him no. He said as he

had no children he could love me as his own child;
he insisted I must not leave him. He would give
me double wages if that would do any good. But
I could not stay. I felt I must go home and tell
my parents, brothers and sister, the glorious news
of redeeming love which I had heard and seen and
talked and felt; if peradventure any of my dear
kindred might believe also, and taste, that the Lord
is gracious. How glad will my dear parents be
when they hear me tell what great things the Lord
has done for my soul. How glad will they be when
they find me a changed, converted boy, regenerated
by God the Holy Ghost, and called by Jesus Christ,
my precious Lord; to know that God in Christ hath
blotted out my sins and remembered them against
me no more forever. How glad will they be when
they hear me tell that Jesus had indeed appeared to
me on my way to Emden to Aurich, appeared to
me when I was sinking into hell. I thought they
would rejoice with me to hear me tell how the lost
was found, how the dead was made alive; to hear
me declare how repentance was given me by Christ,
and obtained by me, a worthless worm. What
change! Oh, what change had God wrought!

Such and many more of like thoughts came over
me when I was working with the aforesaid. The
thought of bringing glad tidings of great joy to my
kindred in the flesh overbalanced everything, and
I quit work to travel some 50 miles a foot without

sleeping, eager to arrive at home once more, *now* to publish the truth of God's forgiving love. When I came near the house of my parents I heard some loud talking in the room. Father had some of his friends with him, and they were in liquor, smoking and talking. I opened the door, went to where father was and said: "Father, the prodigal has come home." "Prodigal, indeed!" said he. "Yes, father," I said, "I am a different boy now from what I used to be. Oh, believe me, Jesus has met me by the way I came from Emden to Aurich. He hath changed me altogether, and he also hath forgiven me my sins. Now you will see me cast down no more, nor will you see me neglecting my business any more. What God has done for me is most wonderful indeed." Speechless the whole company were, listening to my story. Some looked like they were ready to say, "This is an idle tale." Others looked astonished. Mother and sister, who had also come in, were crying, and when I was through telling, father said: "Well, go to bed now, we shall inquire of this matter to-morrow." So the next morning father asked me to tell again what I had told them last night. I told them all before all his workmen too. My father said, "That must be some kind of delusion, and he hoped I would not try to make out that the Apostles' days had returned. That day had passed, said he, and I must have been dreaming it all."

My disappointment was great. I verily had
thought, when my folks heard all, they could not
help believing. I was mistaken. They did not
understand my speech, but unspeakable happiness
and the full assurance of faith in the truths I had
experienced abode with me for some time. I became very attentive to conversations of religious
people, and whenever I could get into their company I was watching very closely, desirious to hear
some one tell something as I had experienced it; of
the plague of sin in the heart, of soul-troubles almost overwhelming, of groanings that cannot be
uttered, of longing desires to know more of Christ.
But I found not one of that kind for several years,
and such as have not experienced, by woeful experience, what sin is, can never know what deliverence
or forgiveness of sin is. What I then chiefly found
among men professing godliness was what one ought
to do, what one's duty was to do, and men dead in
sin were exhorted to do things they knew nothing
about.

Now, as a journeyman tailor, I traveled and
worked awhile in Elberfield, which was said to be
a religious city in the main. I searched for a companion in the love and truth of God, but found
none. Krummacher, a great divine in the Protest-
ant church, preached there. I had read many of
his sermons formerly, and now had a great desire
to hear him preach. I went to his church several

times, but could not get in ; standing room as well as pews were literally packed with people. Now all this time I had come to the conclusion that I was alone in the world with such an experience as mine was. Yet I could have fellowship with prophets and apostles—their experience had been like mine. All had obtained like precious faith. All live unto God and encompass us as a great cloud of witnesses; we find them in the word, sometimes weeping and sometimes rejoicing, sometimes groaning and at other times singing, sometimes in the dark and then again in the light of God's countenance, all looking to Jesus the author and finisher of their faith. Thus God kept up the work of faith in my heart. And thus I was enabled to live unto God also, the faith he had given me being a living faith, pointed continually to the finished work of Christ, and so that living faith and living works of Christ came together, and faith, *with* the works of Christ in me, was not dead. Praise the Lord, oh my soul.

CHAPTER. V.

When the time had come that I must go to another large city to complete my years as a journeyman tailor, according to the laws of that country, I left Elberfield, being intent to go to Hanover, the capitol.

But the Lord had determined otherwise, as I never
arrived in Hanover. Within twelve miles of the
place I fell sick. On the way I felt a weariness
come over me; I sat down on the side of the road.
While I was thinking I was tired only, I meant to
rest a little while, and looking over a valley to a
hill opposite, these words came to me: And I looked
and lo a lamb stood on the mount Zion. Rev. 14: 1.
And verily a beautiful lamb I saw, and a thought
struck me: This is the Lamb of God as it had been
slain. I took my Testament out of my pocket, and
turned to Revelations and found the words. Looking up again, the lamb was there yet. After gazing
awhile upon this wonderful revelation, I commenced
reading again to see what was said about this Lamb
of God. It left a deep impression on me, so deep
that at the time of this writing (1882) it is all as
fresh in my memory as if it had occurred yesterday, though more than thirty-five years ago this
took place.

But my strength failed me, and I could get no
further on my journey. A man, having in charge
a team for marketing, coming that way saw me and
asked me if I was sick? I told him I thought not,
may be I was tired only. He, however, insisted that
I should be helped in his wagon to the nearest town,
called Springe, where I might rest, he said in the
inn. Arriving there, I had become so weak that I
could hardly walk. The kind innkeeper imme-

diately discovered that I was very sick. They wished
to know where I was from, and I could not get my
passport and other papers out of my pocket. So
they conveyed me to a bedroom and sent for a doctor and a magistrate. The physician examined me,
and the magistrate my papers, (as they afterwards
told me) for I had become unconscious as soon as
they had brought me to the bed. My parents were
now informed of all this, and correspondence was
kept up between the parties, and the physician was
besought from various sides to do all in his power,
to try all his skill to save me, etc. But vain is the
help of man. They did all they could for me, in
every way, but for several weeks the physician could
give no encouragement, and at last he gave me up,
and that night they pronounced me dead! They
had supposed I was a Catholic and a priest had been
sent for to manage the funeral. They had ordered
the coffin to be made, and had thought of burying
me in two days. The next morning a lady came
in the room to see the poor dead body, and she examined me and declared there was yet life in me.
The doctor was sent for in haste. He arrived and
said he did not believe it. But this lady implored
him, by the prayers of my parents, to try all in his
power, leave nothing untried, if peradventure I
might be given back, as it were, from the dead, and
the doctor set to work with a will. In less than five
minutes, they said, I had moved my fingers, and

2

then the doctor exclaimed: "The boy is saved! He will live! I'll vouch for the next thirty years for his health!"

During this severe spell of sickness, called nervous fever (Typhus), I was continually in a state of delirium. I fancied that all my relations were dead, and I had no one on earth that would care for me in the future, and while this fancy had settled upon my wandering mind, I saw nothing but desolation and ruin before me. When I was well enough to hear and understand, the folks told me how, previous to my supposed demise, they had to watch me so close. I had repeatedly tried to jump out of the bed. I then recollected plainly how I had seen the door of my room open, and had seen the Lord Jesus Christ come in the room and three or four of his disciples with him. The Lord (for I knew him) came to my bed, laid his hand on my head, and said: "Fear not, thou shalt see thy relatives again." I tried to rise and fall at his feet, but the waiters caught me, and I did not fall on the floor. Oh, blessed Saviour! Let me be nothing, and less than nothing, but, oh permit me to bless thy name for ever and ever. Amen.

In two weeks I thought I felt strong enough to travel on towards home. I was now doubly assured that my father and mother lived; and brothers and sister too. The promise of Jesus was with me, and a letter I had received, with all the well known signatures of all my nearest kindred and relations. Too eager I was now to start home at the earliest possible moment. The folks told me so many things I had said, and all of such a deep religious nature. In the most endearing terms I had almost constantly been preaching, " My beloved Jesus." I was a wonder to them, and every one seemed to rejoice to see me getting well again. Daily I requested the physician to allow me to go home now. At last he consented. It was so arranged that they sent me to Bremen by omnibus, and from thence I must get home as best I might. So I parted from the dear people who had done so much for me; they wept and cried, and fell on my neck and kissed me, and I never saw any of them any more.

" But now thus saith the Lord that created thee, O Jacob, and he that formed thee, O Israel. Fear not, for I have redeemed thee, I have called thee by thy name; thou art mine. When thou passest through the waters, I will be with thee; and through the rivers, they shall not overflow thee. When thou walkest through the fire thou shalt not be burned, neither shall the flame kindle upon thee; for I am the Lord thy God, the Holy One of Israel, thy Saviour." Isaiah 43: 1—3.

Arriving at the place where the stage-driver had his orders to put me off (Bremen), I was to undertake to walk from Bremen to Oldenburg, some thirty miles; from thence to be conveyed again to Leer, Ostfriesland, and finally to Weener where my parents lived. I took my napsack and tried to walk, but found I could not travel on foot. Seeing an inn on the public road where I was creeping along, I went in and told the landlord I could get no farther, and had to at least remain over night; may be I might feel stronger the next morning. I showed him my papers, and he made immediately ready for me to lie down. He told me the authorities ought *not* to have sent me on such a journey; I was in danger of falling into a relapse, and no one could tell the consequence. At least I would not be able to leave his place for many days. He conducted me to a neat little bedroom all to myself, and retir- ing I tried to sleep, but could not. While medita- ting on my condition, I heard the door of my bed- room opened by some one, and my landlord and a stranger stepped into the room. Talking to the stranger, the landlord said: "There is a very sick boy." The stranger said: "Well, I will take him along and bring him to his parents, for I know his parents well." Of course I could not make out what they were talking about, but my heart beat so loud that I could hear it. I looked up, and wished to know what they meant. Then mine host explained to me, that a few minutes ago this gentleman had arrived at the inn with a carriage and two fine horses; had no notion of stopping, when some irre- sistible persuasion had taken hold of him to stop at this place for the night, though he meant to travel some farther on. This man now was to take me in his carriage all the way home, and travelled through the very town where I resided when at home ; that he knew my parents well, and was quite willing to take me along in the morning, provided I might feel strong enough to endure the fatigues of a long ride. Moreover, he said there is in the carriage a comfortable bed, and everything is fixed for such a sick but convalescent boy as you are. I could not answer the man a word. I broke down in tears, and turned around with praise to God and thanksgiving in my heart. And a sweet, refreshing sleep drowned the wonderful intelligence, and the next morning they assisted me to get ready, and bedded me in that fine conveyance of his, and I felt quite comfortable. Now I asked the man how it had come to pass for him to be there at the right time for me? He told me he had been conveying his master to the Insane Asylum at Hanover, and was now back on his way home. And he was glad, he said, to have found me rather than go home all by himself. Verily goodness and mercy have followed me all the days of my life !

"Oh for a heart to praise my God,
A calm and heavenly frame ;
A light to shine upon the road
That leads me to the Lamb."

There was great rejoicing when I reached home. My parents at first sight wept on my neck. They said I had become such a skeleton, and the Lord God be praised, said they, for having spared me. I soon revived under the kind care of my parents.

CHAPTER VI.

When the time had come that I had to be a soldier, I was fully restored to health and strength.
I went in the service at twenty. While in the service
I found a few God-fearing comrades who assembled
nights and Sundays, either in some garret, or in
the woods for worship, all by themselves. This little band I followed and they permitted me to be
with them, to sing and pray, and to listen to what
their speaker and all of them had to say in their experience pertaining to the kingdom of God. Rather
than go to church falsely so-called, I followed these,
my comrades. I loved and sought their company,
because (as I thought) they loved the Lord Jesus
Christ. My dependence upon God I felt daily, and
I loved the few who also felt their weakness. One
of the young men called on me to pray in the assem-
bly. It was the first time I had ever been called
upon to pray. And we all knelt down, and I repeated the prayer which the Lord Jesus had taught
his disciples to pray: "Our Father, which art in
heaven," etc. When we arose from prayer, the
preacher said: "That for one to pray that prayer,
he must have a sure evidence of his sonship, ere he
might say in spirit and in truth, "Our Father."
What! call God our Father without His authority?
Without knowing he is born of God?" I had never

told these believers what I knew of Christ, but some of them said they had heard I had been with Jesus and had been taught of him. Being all of us brought up in the same form of religious worship as it was called, viz: Reformers from the Lutherans, these few men had found out by the Scriptures (and I hope by revelation too) that believers' baptism by immersion was the only and true baptism, and not infant sprinkling or unbelievers' immersion either. As soon as they might be permitted to get home again (there being no Baptists in these parts of the kingdom,) they should immediately make application to the Baptist church for baptism by immersion, and so follow the Lord in His blessed ordinance in obedience to His command.

Now it came to pass that my captain heard of our meetings, and I being the only one of his company who attended them, he sent for me to come to his office immediately. Not knowing, of course, what he wanted, I hastened to his presence. The captain said: "I have heard you visit clandestine meetings of a religious or sectarian kind; is not our church good enough for you fellows to attend? For what purpose are your meetings—and why don't you attend church?" I said: "Mr. Captain, (Herr Hauptmann) because these young men love the Lord Jesus Christ, I have chosen their company. In the church we find no such preaching, praying and singing as among these, God's poor—" He interrupted me, exclaiming, "Fellow, are you crazy? Let me not hear another word of it! About, face! forward, march!" Thus, he commanded me out of his presence. I had made bold in declaring these things to him, because he was about to get married to a preacher's daughter, so peradventure he might love to hear the truth. But he never asked again about it, nor was I ever forbidden to meet with the little band of beloved brethren, though I counted myself unworthy to be with them.

The war with Denmark (1849) called the old soldiers to the front, while we, the recruits of 1848, had to remain in garrison until sufficiently drilled, then to be sent afterward to join the regiment. Thus we were separated, and I never saw any of them again, except one, to whom I shall have occasion to refer to in another place. When we were sent to join the regiment, peace was declared; while we were quartered at Zelle for a few months, though I found no people nor any companion in the fear of God in the place, I experienced some powerful and sweet manifestations of the loving kindness of our God. The Saviour was made very precious to my heart occasionally, that I could at times exclaim: "Precious, precious Jesus! O let my heart be thy dwelling, as thou hast been my dwelling place through all generations!" I have at times felt such a nearness to the Lord, that when by myself I have wept tears of joy: continually blessing and praising the name of Jesus; but, oh, when these short moments end, though not quite quite left alone, I miss the presence of my friend like one whose comforts are gone.

> "I to my own sad place return,
>   My loneliness to feel ;
> I sigh, I pant, I groan and mourn,
>   And am but barren still,"

So I prayed in the spirit of that blessed Word :

> "More frequent let thy visits be,
>   Or let them longer last ;
> I can do nothing without Thee,
>   Make haste, my God, make haste!"

A short time after this, we were sent home on furlough.

CHAPTER VII.

I now being twenty-two years of age, got married, and after one year's stay in the place where my wife's parents resided, (Nienburg,) I emigrated to my country, Weener, with my wife and child. A few days only had we been at the home of my parents, when I heard father's foreman tell him concerning a new sect being started (as they called it) in our town, consisting of a few men and some old women, perhaps some ten or twelve persons, all told. They were excluded from the Missionary Baptist church, because they had believed that salvation was of

grace alone, and now they had organized and had a
minister ordained over them by one of the Holland
Grace Baptists, and in fact they now talked of nothing else but free grace—free grace and Jesus Christ.
They had quit drinking liquor altogether, and they
cursed and swore no more at all, and one of the
worst drunkards had also united with them, and he
a tailor too.   And he was said to be one of the ablest
to talk of free grace, and such things, as if they were
the elect and the only ones to be saved, etc., etc.   I
trembled when I heard that man tell these things to
my father.   I could not stay in the same room any
longer.   I went out of the shop to where I could be
entirely by myself.   Weeping, I cried to the Lord,
saying, "O Lord, this is the people I so long have
sought; O lead me to this people."   Now I made
up my mind to go and see the worst one of that
crowd (as they were called) as soon as my day's work
was done.   That same night I went.   His wife, who
was at that time bitterly opposed to his faith, was
not at home, the children were in bed, and he was
entirely by himself, reading in the Bible.   When I
came in, he shut the book, and after a " Good evening, sir," I said to him, " We had a nice day to-day."
" Oh, yes," said he, " Our God is good ; he causes his
sun to shine over the good and over the evil; he
gives rain to the just and unjust.   But we by nature
are ever so ungrateful, and are trampling his goodness continually under our unhallowed feet."   I gave
vent to tears, and told him that such alas ! was my

case exactly. Now this man's mother was a godly
person, and in times past I had told her what the
Lord Jesus had done for a mad Gaderene like I had
been, and the dear old lady had told her son, after
he had come to a knowledge of the Lord. This I
was told afterward. When he saw me weeping, now
for the first time I was with him, he wept too, and
then commenced preaching Jesus to me, just as I
loved to hear it: for so I had been taught my adorable Saviour by the Lord himself, just so he had
revealed himself to me and in me, in short the man
spake to me as never man had spoken to me before.
And when he said, " Let us pray," we knelt down on
the brickstone floor, and he prayed forth the prayer
and praise with fervency and supplication such as I
had never heard before from any man. O happy
hour to me ! I felt in my soul the magnifying power
of the Lord, and my spirit did rejoice in God my
Saviour, for he had regarded the low estate of his
servant, and had set me among the princes of his
kingdom. Here I could sit at Jesus' feet. This was
the gate of heaven. It was heaven in my heart,
heaven around, above and beneath. Heaven and
happiness were wafted through my every bone and
marrow. Verily, O Lord, in thy presence is fullness
of joy ! And to thee, O most precious Saviour, to
thee be honor and power everlasting. Amen.

When I started home the dear man grasped me by
the hand, and said he felt it in his heart that I was
his dear brother, and with blessings trembling on

his lips, he uttered a "God bless you," and sent me
away, and I went home rejoicing. This was my
first truly happy time I had ever spent with one of
God's humble poor, yea, one of the most despised of
that little flock—despised by the world because the
grace of God worked in him mightily, and with
boldness he declared that Jesus is the Christ, the
same yesterday, to-day and forever, and salvation to
the uttermost in Jesus and none other. His name
was Wert Broons. When I got home I told my wife
I had been to see the man of whom she had heard
so much to-day. She thought it was almost crim-
inal in me to have done so. I told her, that bad as
the man had been formerly, he now was a good
man. Grace had made him good. Now Christ was
living in that man. But my wife being a stranger
in the place could not understand why it was that
my parents could be so set against the men they
called Grace Baptists. So she told my parents that
I had been to see that dangerous man. Then my
father took me aside and in the presence of mother
told me that they were informed I had been to see
a man who had gone over to that despised little sect,
and if that ever came to the ears of our pious customers, they would never forgive me, and I need
not look for patronage from them in my business.
He (father) entreated me not to have anything more
to do with that crowd. Stay or abide in the church
where you were baptized (sprinkled) in infancy and

confirmed in youth. These Baptists, poor fellows, have departed from the faith of Luther, and of all our great and pious reformers, and in their delusion they suppose they are better than all of us. Yes, no man cares for them; and if you ever should get the disease of attaching yourself to them, you will have to starve and go begging, and all the schooling (education) I gave you, said father, will be entirely thrown away on you. Will you now ruin yourself and little family for no cause? Take warning in time, and remember that it can make you in no wise better than you are now. You are now as good a christian as you ever need to be. Don't meddle with this thing, or else they will have you under the water.

But God in his mercy directed my mind to his word. Then I learned that it is far better to follow the Lord than to listen to the reasonings of any man. The more I became acquainted with the Baptists that advocated sound doctrine and lived worthy of the gospel, the more I loved them. Indeed, I could say in the words of Scripture: "Of whom the world was not worthy." However, it soon was noised abroad that I visited several of that sect everywhere spoken against, and I was regarded with suspicion by all who knew I leaned that way, though at that time I had not as much as thought upon the subject of baptism by immersion. The brethren had not called

my attention to it. It was their opinion that the
Lord himself must reveal this also to a believer.
One night the baptism of our Lord Jesus Christ
came in vision to my understanding, and then for
the first time I discovered that I, who for years had
professed to love and to follow the Lord, had not
followed him in his ordinance of baptism by immersion. O Lord, I cried, is this for me? O reveal
it to me; make it plain to me, and enable me to
follow thee in all thy commands. In the morning
I began searching the Scriptures upon this particular subject, and, behold, look where I might, I found
it written as with a sunbeam. I asked the Lord, if
consistent with his holy will, to permit me to be
with his dear people, to make it plain to me, and if
infant sprinkling was according to his word it must
be right; if not, it must be false doctrine, a delusion,
an error. And if believers' baptism (immersion) was
according to his word, I begged His Majesty to reveal it to me with power sufficient for me to declare,
What hindereth me to be baptized ? And the Lord
rewarded my diligent search with the full assurance
that believers' baptism only was according to his
word and revelation. Oh, the nights and days of
longing! When I was satisfied upon this point,
then the question came up, Was I worthy? Had I
not neglected the ordinance too long? Still, the
desire to be baptized by immersion, and thus be

united to God's dear people, increased day by day.
Again and again I heard, as though one spoke to
me, " Why tarriest thou? Arise and be baptized in
the name of the Lord."

Some six or eight miles from our town was, or is,
a city called Leer. A little congregation of baptized
believers assembled at the house of one whose name
was Termœhlen. One Sunday morning early it was
impressed on my mind that I must go to their meeting. Accordingly I started and walked thither, and
arrived in time for preaching to commence. The
meeting lasted the whole day, and towards evening
I started for home again, when the minister said he
would accompany me a few miles on my way. Now
to the minister I unburdened my mind, and I heard
from him the same blessed truth, concerning baptism by immersion, as I had been taught it by revelation. And, indeed, I exclaimed and said: Lo!
here is water, what hindereth me to be baptized?
He said there was a congregation of brethren in our
town, and when they assembled I might tell them
all I had told him, and when they all were satisfied,
he would baptize me. But oh, brother, saith he,
consider—prayerfully consider, the trials and tribu-
lations which await you when you take this step.
You may be forsaken of father and mother; your
brothers also will turn against you; your wife may
leave you; your customers will cease to patronize
you, and you may very likely be reduced to poverty

and want. Do you think you can stand all this?
I said, with fear and trembling: "The Lord will provide." Then he grasped me by the hand, his eyes
filled with tears, and he said: "The Lord bless you,
my dear brother. For my part, I am satisfied.

CHAPTER VIII.

" The opening heavens 'round me shine,
    With beams of sacred bliss,
  While Jesus shows his heart is mine,
    And whispers I am his."

How shall I describe the feelings I had upon the
manifestation of being found worthy to follow my
blessed Master into the watery grave? To be buried
with him by baptism into his death? The verse I
just quoted I knew nothing of at that time, yet the
words fell this morning with sweetness in my heart,
and I apply them here because they were then
wholly applicable to my case. I was, as it were, carried along above earth and earthly things. I found
the Lord Jesus precious to my soul, the chief among
ten thousand, the one altogether lovely. It now
spread among God's dear poor, that I was by grace
a fit candidate for baptism.

One evening (Thursday) word was sent me, the
preacher had come, and the little congregation was

to meet at eight o'clock. I went, too, and related to the little flock what I then knew, and I was received to be baptized that night. When on our way toward the water, the minister remarked that it seemed to him there was a little something in the way, that I seemed to be in the dark or under a cloud, because I had become so uncommunicative all at once. Then I told him that I had promised my preacher, who had severely questioned or catechised me, whenever the Lord should make it manifest to me that believers' baptism by immersion was for me and according to scripture, I was to let him know it, ere I was baptized. Then our ministering brother said: "Brother Greenwood, we cannot baptize you tonight. First of all, let that gentleman know that you are fully persuaded. He that believeth shall not make haste." Then the cloud vanished, and I was glad. Now, the brethren appointed another night for the solemn ordinance, but I said: "Brethren, let me be baptized in day-time." Such a thing as baptizing in broad daylight had not as yet been tried. Even at nights they had sometimes been disturbed by enemies. Men armed with shotguns or pockets full of rocks had attempted to drive apart the little bands, and had also frequently threatened the life of the minister. When on this occasion the brethren stood in doubt as to the propriety or impropriety of adopting my suggestion, I said: "Brethren, let me be baptized in daylight: *Jesus reigns.*" Then said they: "The will of the Lord be done." And Sunday morning, ten o'clock, was the hour appointed for us all to be at the water. This was on Thursday night.

On Friday morning I informed the preacher whom I had promised, that upon prayerful searching of God's word, and by revelation of Jesus Christ, my Lord, I was fully persuaded that believers' baptism was the commandment of Christ to his people, and to me. I now said nothing at all upon the subject to any one, not even to my wife. When Sunday morning had come, my wife seemed pleased, because for two days past I had said not a word one way or another upon the much talked-of subject, baptism. She said she hoped I had quit the notion altogether. I told her, No; I felt that I should have grace given me to follow my Lord. She asked if I would tell her when it was to be? I replied, " No, my dear, I will not. You might raise up an army of Satan's host, to disturb and give us trouble." About half an hour after this, I dressed for the purpose of going out, and my wife wanted me to take our little boy along, (then about two years old.) I had no objections. I took the child by the hand, and leisurely strolled through the streets, until I got out of the town. Then I took the babe in my arms, and walked faster to be in time where the brethren had appointed at the water-side. I once turned to see around me, and lo, a woman was following me, I now feared this person might make trouble. I breathed a longing prayer to the Lord for his mercy, when the woman turned around, left, and I saw her no more. In the distance I saw the brethren at the water. My heart sang praises to God. Upon arrival I changed apparel the brethren had brought for me, and the brother minister took me by the hand and led me into the water. He spoke the solemn words: " According to the commandment of our dear Lord and Saviour, Jesus Christ, I baptize thee in the name of the Father, and of the Son, and of the Holy Ghost. Amen!" I realized that I had been buried and now risen with Jesus, and exclaimed aloud: " Now I am thine, O Lord Jesus, entirely thine own. Hallelujah! Amen."

Filled with exceeding great joy, I now bent towards home, and the brethren, too, went in different directions toward their abodes. On my way I took my little boy into a friend's house, who had told us to come over some time and get some cherries. I helped the child climb the tree, and he picked the cherries himself, and filled his little handkerchief with the fruit. Coming home he was delighted to tell his mother how he himself had plucked the cherries, and thus (as I had desired it) he had his mind altogether on this one thing. Dinner being just ready we sat down to dinner. I was enabled to

lisp forth a short but fervent prayer, and during
mealtime my wife remarked :

"I think there must be something unusual the
matter with you, for I have not seen you so cheer-
ful for some time." However, I said nothing, and
told her only how pleased our little boy had been
when he picked the cherries off the tree. In the
afternoon my wife expected me to go to church (so-
called), because my favorite preacher was to preach,
but I declined, not giving any reason for declining.

After service grandmother came over and de-
manded a reason for my absence. I gave none,
however, but she looked at me with suspicion. When
the evening bells began to ring, grandmother said :
"Now, come along. Go to church and fill your seat."
She grasped me by the arm and pulled me along,
when I said : "Grandmother, its no use. I shall go
to church no more; that is, I am *done with Babylon
forever.*" Oh ! the looks the dear old lady gave me !
She turned to my wife and said at once: "Then he
is baptized." My wife was astonished. She came
right straight before me and said : "Are you baptized?" I said : "Yes, my dear, I am baptized." She
ran out of the house like one crazy, crying repeatedly: "My husband is baptized !" Some of the old
friends of the reformed church took her in, and told
her it was no crime, she ought not to act thus, etc.
She, however, was determined she would leave me,
and would live with me no longer. My own rela-

tives had told her it certainly might be better for any one to be sent to the penitentiary for a few years, than to be baptized by that low set of Baptists.

She went also to my parents, and said she was determined to leave me. But they told her no. We were married, and now she had better try to bear with me for weal or woe. Father and one of my brothers brought her home, but she refused to be comforted. "Now you can go preaching," were the first words father spoke when he came in, "then you sure must starve your little family." I took the Bible, and where it fell open I read, and said: Oh, that I might have this ministry, receive mercy and faint not. I read Cor. 2: 1, 4, 10. Also we are to give no offence in anything, that the ministry be not blamed, but in all things approving ourselves as the ministers of God in much patience, in afflictions, in necessities, in distresses, in stripes, in imprisonment, in tumults, in labors, in watchings, in fastings, by pureness, by knowledge, by long suffering, by kindness, by the Holy Ghost, by love unfeigned, by the word of truth, by the power of God, by the armor of righteousness on the right hand and on the left, by honor and dishonor, by evil report and good report; as deceivers, and yet true; as unknown, and yet well known; as dying, behold we live; and chastened and not killed; as sorrowing, yet always rejoicing; as poor, yet making many rich; as having nothing, yet possessing all things.

2 Cor. 6: 3, 10. Here I closed the book. Then
came the wife of Dr. Broons in the room ; taking
father aside, she said: "Mr. G., the preacher who bap‑
tized your son, is in our house, let us have him ar‑
rested." Father said : "No, madam ; I am no Judas.
That preacher is blameless. My son—it is all my
son's fault; he ought to have known better." The
next day my wife was preparing to leave me. I
went over to brother B., and told him what I feared.
He opened the Bible and read : "And unto the mar‑
ried I command, yet not I, but the Lord, Let not the
wife depart from her husband, * * but if the unbe‑
lieving depart, let him depart. A brother or a sis‑
ter is not under bondage in such cases, but God hath
called us to peace;" and there is one thing that
you can do, said our brother, "that is for you not in
any wise give occasion for offence, nor permit that
apprentice of yours to help her off." When I came
home my wife was calling on the boy to go to the
office and have the driver of the stage or omnibus
to stop for her, when I said : "No, he shall not go;
but one thing let me tell you, my dear little wife,
you have now given place to Satan so long, and if
you keep on in this way, he will soon have you in
hell." She threw off her fixings, and sat down and
wept, and then she turned her face to me and said :
"Bernard, forgive me ; and tell all your brethren,
and ask their forgiveness for me ; I have done all
of you a grievous wrong." I saw she was sincere.

The Lord had quieted her. The Lord had triumphed gloriously, and I had occasion to praise his great and wondrous name. Praise ye the Lord!

CHAPTER IX.

Since it had pleased God to restore my wife's con-fidence in me, he gave me also a grateful heart, and enabled me to endure the sneers and neglects of kindred and strangers, and my most gracious Lord condescended to keep me in his fear, and caused me to find him precious above all that might be named. His grace (Oh the blissful theme!) was sufficient for me to stand, upheld by his righteous, omnipotent hand. Day by day have I learned what is meant by worshipping God in spirit and have no confidence in the flesh. By sad experience I have heard also that in me, that is in my flesh dwells no good thing. When I would do good evil is present. I am carnal, sold under sin. My best thoughts, my best inten-tions, and the best that I can do are so polluted, that unwashed in Jesus' blood, they would sink me down to perdition, but I am not giving to the church the history of my life. Were I called upon to do that, and were I to undertake the task, it would be as im-possible as it would be unprofitable. In this I am trying tell my Father's sons and daughters and my

mother's children in the faith of God's elect, what
my God and their God has done for me. What de-
liverances from dead weights, from sickness, sorrow,
grief and pain the dear Saviour manifested to me.
What separation from a professing and profane world
had to take place. When my heart had, as it were,
been rent in sunder, what peace, what comfort Jesus
has given me! I am trying to tell of the love visits
of Immanuel Jesus to me, of the many tears he has
wiped from off my face. O blessed God, thanks be
unto Thee; God himself shall wipe away all tears
from our eyes. Oh ye disconsolate, that weep for
sin and over a suffering Saviour. Take courage!
The Lord is faithful. He will never leave you or
forsake you. Yes, I want to tell you how he always
hears and answers the groanings of his poor sin-
smitten people, and tell you of the whispers of his
love, of his forgiving mercy, of the washing of regeneration, (if I wash thee not thou hast no part
with me,) of the blood of Christ applied to a sinner
as vile as I am, of the promises he promised and
fulfilled, and of the sprinkling of the blood of the
Son of God that speaketh eternal things in the heart
by God the Holy Ghost! Oh, beloved, bear with
me a little while longer; I have come before you in
this book with no other intent than to show you as
well as I can the super-abounding grace of our
Lord Jesus Christ. Rom. 5: 20. To whom be
glory, honor and dominion for ever and ever. Amen.

Immediately after my baptism I felt I had obtained the answer of a good conscience toward God. I felt the drawings of eternal love to Jesus' feet. For a whole week Satan was not permitted to disturb or trouble me in the least. Night and day I enjoyed sweet communion with my beloved. "As the apple tree is among the trees of the wood, so is my beloved among the sons. I sat down under his shadow with great delight, and his fruit was sweet to my taste. He brought me to his banqueting house and his banner over me was love." Cant. 2: 3, 4. And with the bride, the Lamb's wife, I was enabled to exclaim and say: Thou art fairer than the children of men; grace is poured into thy lips, therefore God hath blessed thee forever. Ps. 45: 2. I could rejoicingly meditate on God's everlasting love. I was often lost in wonder at the amazing depths, and heights, and lengths of it, having reached unto me the vilest of the vile. Oh the depth of the riches, both of the love and knowledge of our God! How unsearchable are His judgments and his ways past finding out. I feasted upon the sufferings, the body and blood of Christ, with indescribable peace. I feasted upon my Saviour's triumphant resurrection, whom angels adore and upon his word saying, I am Alpha and Omega, the beginning and the ending. I am he that was dead and and am alive forevermore, and have the keys of hell and of death. Unto whom is given all power in heaven and in

3

earth; and with pleasing wonder and delight I have
been enabled to exclaim, O Lord take me now
unto thyself! It is enough! I want to see thee as
thou art! Thou art my heaven, my all. I want no
more. Glory hallelujah. Amen.

But my prayer was answered in God's way. Elijah
was told there were seven thousand besides him that
had not bowed the knee to Baal. And to Paul it
was said, My grace is sufficient for thee.

The Sunday following the Sunday of my baptism
(August, 1853,) I was to realize that my feasting days
were at an end for the time being at least. It was
said to Israel, " Thou shalt observe the feast of taber-
nacles seven days, after that thou hast gathered in
thy corn and thy wine; seven days thou shalt keep
a solemn feast unto the Lord thy God, in the place
which the Lord shall choose; because the Lord thy
God shall bless thee in all thine increase, and
all the works of thine hands, therefore thou shalt
surely rejoice." Deut. 16: 13, 15. " But the days
will come when the bridegroom shall be taken away
from them, and then they fast in those days."
Mark 2: 20.

I went to meeting with the brethren that day and
all of a sudden

> "I missed the presence of my friend,
> Like one whose comfort's gone."

I was in distress such as I had never felt upon
me before—darkness so great I could see nothing

at all. Where were the delights I had previous to
this moment seen and known, and felt to be in Jesus ?
What had become of my joys and rejoicings? Where
was the beauty I had been made to see in the little
handful of worshipping, believing children of the
living God? They now looked to me like a root
out of dry ground. Had I been mistaken, deluded,
deceived ? Others seemed to be at liberty, and that
made me the more sensibly feel my bondage. What
could be the matter with me? I did feel neither
lost nor saved. I felt cold, barren and desolate. I
tried to call to mind my past communion season
with my dearest Lord, but all in vain. My heart
felt as hard as the nether mill-stone. I thought I
surely must have grasped the shadow and missed
the substance. Now I mourned sore like a dove be-
reft of its mate. I groaned till I was weary with
groaning. I cried to God in language of the Psalmist : " Return, O Lord, deliverer of my soul : oh save
me for thy mercies' sake. For in death there is no
remembrance of thee : in the grave who shall give thee
thanks?" Psa. 6 : 4, 5. My Saviour had withdrawn
his face. I was most miserable. Satan would sug-
gest: You are nothing but a hypocrite after all ;
you are an enthusiast anyhow. O I was brought
very low. In times past I had been able to bless the
Lord for the forgiveness of all my sins. I had praised
God with songs of thanksgiving and melody in the
heart. Whither had my dearest Lord gone? Did

I not know in whom I had believed? Wist I not
that his love toward me had been better to me than
life, strong as death, quenching the flames of hell
for wretched me, and drowning all my abominable
sins in the blood of the Lamb? All, all this was at
a distance now. I knew I must return unto the
Lord, but how to return I found not. My heart was
unfeeling, prayer was a burden, and to think upon
the name of God always was not in my power. I
had thought I would convince others and bring
souls to Christ. From this zeal, which was not according to knowledge, I was completely stripped,
and the ragged clothing of creature goodness, creature ability was torn off of me, and I saw myself a
helpless, leprous and loathsome sinner in God's sight
and to the King I could not come myself, much less
lead or bring others to him. How could I tell of
Jesus and his love, if God had been pleased to shut
my mouth? Unless I could feel in my heart what
the Lord had done for me, I always had to remain
at a distance, silent and dumb before God. And
now his hand in providence seemed to be against
me. Satan beset me hard. Ah, said he, "where is
now thy God?" At this time I had not a friend in
the world. I had come out of it and left all behind.
United to a few God had formed for himself, they
differed from the religious and irreligious, from the
professing and profane world all the same. The
separation that had taken place I felt was final, and

I had chosen to be with the loved ones whom the
Lord calls his poor and afflicted people; as it is
written, "I will leave in the midst of thee a poor and
afflicted people and they *shall* trust in the *name* of
the Lord." And now while reviewing the battle-
field, I am constrained to say with one of old : "If
it had not been the Lord who was on our side when
men rose up against us, then the waters had overwhelmed us, the stream had gone over our souls."
But in the days of my darkness and distress, I had
now and then the liberty feelingly to exclaim :
"Though he slay me, yet will I trust in him." O what
is this life worth without Jesus Christ ?

Fellow-sinner, suffer the word of exhortation. Life
without Christ in you is but misery and death. I
have found it so, and if the Lord had not bestowed
his all-sufficient grace upon me in the day of my
calamity, I should have been with devils in hell. But
the Holy Ghost made me cry to the Lord, in the
language of the singer in Israel : "Hear, O Lord,
when I cry with my voice, have mercy also upon me
and answer me. When thou saidst: Seek ye my
face, my heart said unto thee ; Thy face, O Lord, will
I seek : Hide not thy face from me, put not thy servant away in anger. Thou hast been my help, leave
not, neither forsake me, O God of my salvation.
When my father and mother forsake me, the Lord
will take me up." Psa. 37 : 7–10. And now they
had forsaken, and the Lord knew. And when at one

time I brought my groaning petition to the mercy
seat of his blessed Majesty, these words were given
as with the voice from heaven in my heart:. "Why
art thou cast down, O my soul, and why art thou
disquieted within me? Hope thou in God, for I
shall yet praise him, who is the health of my countenance and my God." Then the Saviour's sufferings were presented to the eyes of my understanding. Then I began to reason thus: If the with-
drawal of the Saviour's countenance causes a worthless sinner such sore distress, what must my Saviour
himself have felt when his Father hid his face from
him and he cried, "My God, my God, why hast thou
forsaken me?" O ye ends of the earth, ye troubled
ones, and all you that are in distress, who walk in
darkness and have no light, behold and see if there
be any sorrow like unto the sorrow of the Son of
God. He was oppressed and he was afflicted, yet he
opened not his mouth. True we may weep sometimes, but what is our weeping to his strong crying
and tears? I was enabled to trace him from the manger to the cross. *A Saviour slain!* A Saviour slain
for me! This healed me. It brought an immediate
cure, and to this day has helped me in mine often
infirmities. To be led by the Spirit of God feelingly
and experimentally into the birth, life and suffering
of Jesus, to be thus baptized into the death and resurrection of the sin-bearing, sin-atoning, and sin-
destoying Lamb of God, melt the hardest heart, tears

of love, thanksgiving and praise begin to flow ; one
is made partaker of Christ's sufferings, the poor,
heavy laden sinner is made to feel that this blessed
Saviour is able to save to the uttermost—save from
distress, darkness of mind, hardness of heart, and
all manner of abominable sins; to save from foes in-
ternal, external and infernal; to save from death,
hell and destruction, and to snatch him as a brand
from the fire, to set him among princes, to show
him the inheritance that is incorruptible, grace
which directs him to the blood that cleanses from
all sins, applies the same to the sorrowful soul, and
thus causes the heavy laden and sin-burdened soul
to triumph in Christ, and from the dunghill of self-
abasement, the soul exultantly cries: "Who shall
lay anything to the charge of God's elect?" Oh the
love, the power, the sweetness of this glorious truth.
But we all with open faces beholding as in a glass
the glory of the Lord, are changed into the same
image from glory to glory even as by the Spirit
of the Lord. His visits cause the snare of the
fowler to be broken. He speaks at sundry times
and in divers manner. The vision may tarry, yet
wait! It will sure come in God's time and in his
own way. The voice of the Good Shepherd shall
surely reach the ears and hearts too of all his sheep,
and when they hear his voice they will follow him,
through evil as well as through good, though they
be scattered in the cloudy and dark day. We have

cause then to bless his dear name; "as in the days
of his flesh he never did, so now in the day of his
power he never will reject the cry nor refuse the act
of mercy to any who are brought under a conscious sense of their state to look to him." Jesus
says: "Behold, I come quickly!" May the echo of
our heart be: "Even so; come, Lord Jesus, come
quickly."

CHAPTER X.

About this time I took the privilege of going to
meeting every Thursday night and every Sunday.
Sometimes I was pressed down with the cares of life.
But meeting with God's poor at the place of wor-
ship, the brethren seemed to understand my case.
In their prayers, they brought all my wants and
hard cases to Jesus. In union with the loved ones
I too could put down all my troubles at Jesus' feet.

One Sunday morning, when we were assembled
in a small room, the doors being locked, not for fear
of the Jews, but for fear of Christians so called—
some one was heard to knock at the door. Brother
Dickman, the deacon at whose house the meeting
was held, arose to see who might be there, opened
the door, when a deacon of the so called "great
church" (the reformed church,) an elderly man be-

tween fifty and sixty years of age, stepped in the house, whom the brethren had known for many years as a devout man. This man, I say, stepped in the room, and looking upon the company assembled, said: "This is the place. Here is the house of God." He sat down for a little while, and then the brethren requested him to speak freely, whereupon he rose and spoke about as follows:

" Beloved brethren:—For many years I have been panting after God, as the hart panteth after the waterbrooks, and though I have been looked upon and considered by some to be a devout and pious man, yet they did not know what a miserable sinner I was. I felt my sins to be a burden night and day, until one day when I heard some one saying to me: 'Son, be of good cheer, thy sins, which are many, are all forgiven thee.' And with the words came unutterable happiness, and which filled my soul. I then joined the great church as a full member, and still continued there, till I was exalted and set apart by the pastor and members as an elder or deacon. But all the time I have been there, I have felt a strange something I could not account for, and for the first time I heard of you: though I knew none of you, except one or two, my heart was stirred within me, and involuntarily I was drawn in prayer to God, praying that the Lord would lead me to his people. But as God had given me this desire, I could not remain at ease, and when the

preachers and deacons heard of it, they visited me,
and knowing that I am a very poor turf-digger,
they asked me if I would not like to own a cow, a
few hogs, etc.   They said they would give me all
these things, if I would keep away from these Baptists; for they had heard that I had been meditating concerning baptism by immersion.   Now yesterday, while at work all by myself, I heard a voice
speaking to me, saying: 'Arise, and go whither I
show thee.'   The spade dropped from my hands,
and speechless I looked around to see whence the
words had come, when I heard the same words once
more and my mind was directed to a few believing
Baptists, who I thought worshipped God in spirit
and in truth.   Yea, it was in this room, this very
house, this same people, and I in spirit beheld your
order and saw that Christ of a truth is in you.   Immediately I left spade and turf, and went home,
meditating upon the vision.   I tried to go to work
again but could not.   I knew the vision was of the
Lord.   This morning I started to find the place
which thus had been shown to me in spirit, and
coming to your town I went right straight to the
house a little child pointed out to me, when I told
her what house I wanted to go to.   Now, dear people of God, if you will have me, O receive me,
though I am utterly unworthy to be in your company.".

While this brother related the foregoing, we could

not restrain our tears, and then all joined in singing a hymn of praise, united in prayer, and grace
was given, abundant grace, to pour out our hearts
to God in supplicative prayer and praise. O, sweet
moments to sit at Jesus' feet. The dear Lord poured
out his sweet blessings upon the lowly and the
poor. Praise ye the Lord his saints, and bless his
holy name for ever and ever! Praise him in the
sanctuary; praise him in your hearts, praise him
with your lips and lives, and let your whole life be
devoted to his praise! He himself, God the Father,
God the Son, and God the Holy Ghost, the Three-
One God is constantly engaged to pour upon the
house of Israel the Spirit of grace and supplication.
He filleth the poor with good things, and the rich he
sendeth empty away.

This brother was gladly received, and on Thursday night following was baptized (immersed) in the
stream; and subsequently he also gave evidence that
he enjoyed all spiritual things, with the people of
the Lord who have all these things in common.

CHAPTER XI.

On that never-to-be-forgotten Sunday morning,
for the time being of our meeting, I forgot all about
house and home, wife and child. It did not occur

to me that I was to find no dinner on the table, no
meat, no fuel in the house to cook anything with.
Now when I arrived at home I felt my soul had been
fed with the rich food of God's house, but also felt
strange and downhearted at the thought of having
nothing for dear wife and baby to eat. My companion remarked : "You can go to meeting and enjoy yourselves, knowing that we have nothing to eat
at home." I said, "Well, the Lord' is gracious, perhaps he will have mercy on us this day." She said
she thought it did not look like it this time : she
could not comprehend how God could let his children (if they were his children) be brought so low.
"It must be a punishment sent us for your leaving
church," &c. I tried to persuade her that we should
never starve to death, and that I believed the Lord
would even this day give us a plenty of all we needed.
My favorite Psalm (the 42d) was uppermost in my
mind, when one of my former customers stepped in
the room and said: "Mr. Greenwood, I owe you one
dollar (thaler); I thought I might pay it to you just
as well now as at any other time." I thanked him,
and he departed, having laid the silver thaler on
the table. I said to my wife, "What do you say now?
This indeed is the Lord's doing, he was constrained
to pay that debt. Had he had his own way in this
matter, he would not have paid it on Sunday. For
he was then being educated for a Missionary
preacher, and according to their teaching one must

not even pay his debts on Sunday." Now I took the
big basket, (it being between twelve and one o'clock
at noon when the stores are open for the accommodation of the poor), and went and bought everything
we stood in need of, enough to last us several days.
God also gave me a heart to thank him. I magni-
fied and blessed his dear exalted name, and sang the
one hundred and third Psalm, for he had graciously
been pleased to send in the last and only money I
had standing out, just in time of need. All my customers had forsaken me as a covenant-breaker, (for
so they called me; because I had regarded my own
infant sprinkling as null and void), and had thus
forsaken me, yet the dear Lord would sometimes
send in a man from the country to have a garment
made by me, and thus I was not altogether forsaken. It
came to pass that I had made a full suit for an honest
farmer, and one day I expected him to come after it;
but at the time appointed the man did not come.
He was expected to come after the clothes either
that Saturday night or the following Monday morning. But what to do over Sunday we know not.
Should I ask some one to trust us with some things
till Monday morning? No; I was not in the habit
of asking credit of any one, and did not know how
to begin now. Sunday morning came, and the last
piece of bread and the last cup of coffee were thank-
fully enjoyed, and—O the sinfulness of the human
heart—the rebellion of my poor heart was stirred. I

began to murmur at my fate. I fretted because all
these things were against me. I resolved to ask my
parents for the loan of one dollar until Monday
morning, and off I went towards their residence.
Now I had not been in their presence since my baptism, (about six weeks previous,) and my mother
and sister being alone, looked like they were saying,
"Take care. How dare you come here!" However,
I said : "Mother, I wish you would lend me one dollar till to-morrow morning. I will pay it back then."
She answered that she had it not to lend. Then my
sister commenced crying, and said : "O mother,
don't say that you have not the money; do let Bernhard have it, he loves Jesus." But mother gave us
to understand that father would not allow it. While
she was yet speaking, the little girl weeping, father
came in at the front door, and then I went out at
the back-door, hoping he had not seen me. He
asked sister what was the matter, what was she crying about? And the child told him all, and then
looked up to him with a look of confidence, and
said : "Oh, father, give Bernhard a dollar, do." He
said : "Where is he?" "He has just gone out," was
the reply. Immediately he ran out at the same
door by which I had made my escape, called me
back, put his fingers in his vest pocket, and said :
"You want a dollar? Here it is." I told him I
would pay it back to-morrow. He said he had lost
all confidence in me since I had turned Baptist. Oh

how ashamed did I now feel before my God! Had such a thing been possible, I could have crept in the earth. Here I was taught where to look for help, and that all my frettings and murmurings concerning my fate only tended to confusion, darkness, sorrow and distress. The next day early in the morning the man came and paid me a handful of silver, and I hurried back and paid my father. He said he had not looked for it. I understood him, and told him Baptists must "owe no man anything." From that time forth I had sufficient work to prevent our asking favors of any one, which always was a very difficult task for me to do. And some who at first had taken their work from me came back; a few acted as though I ought to thank them for their patronage, and I gave them to understand in christian love that none could come to me with work except God the Father sent them. So Christmas came, and before us was a long winter yet. Gloomy thoughts as to the future stole upon me; I became down-hearted again, and could not even tell the brotherhood how scant we had to live, lest they might feel as to throw in their mite for me which they needed themselves. While thoughts and cares of that kind troubled me not a little, the letter carrier stepped in the room and handed me a letter. I had not the half cent (two pennies) of postage. I succeeded in borrowing it, and then, O wonder! it was a letter from America. I called my wife to listen—and the letter was from my brother John, then living in Cincinnati, Ohio. With trembling hands I opened the letter, and the contents thereof were translated nearly as follows:

" *Dear Brother Bernhard:*

Of late I have had a strong impression on my mind to write a letter to you. You are perhaps now your own master, and have set up in business; but in the fatherland you may work and work until you die, but you will never be any better off in the world than when you first began. A mechanic is but a slave in the old country. If you were here in America you would get well paid for your labor, and you might get along here as easy as the richest men in the old country. I know you will say, I cannot come, not having the means. But if you will tell me you will come, I will send you the money, for you, your wife and child. Write immediately. If you will come, say so."

Wife says, " What shall we do?" I said: " We will go; this is the work of God, blessed be his holy name. America, that highly favored country! where people have liberty to baptize in day time, without being interfered with, and privilege to worship God according to the dictates of his holy word."

CHAPTER XII.

The next morning I wrote to my brother that we were willing, most gladly willing to come to such an highly favored country as America. Told my brother to send money enough for myself and wife, and I thought we might realize money enough for the little boy out of the sale of our furniture. We had not long to wait before a letter came enclosing a draft for the amount I wrote for, which was sixty dollars in American money. Now, when it became known that I was going to leave, father, mother, brothers and sister took it very much to heart : they seemed to have never anticipated such an ending of the drama of my young life in the fatherland. And when it became generally known, I soon had a visit of my former Arminian brethren, who declared that such a thing as leaving one's country was not expedient for a Christian to do. They said that a Christian had no right, according to Scripture, to leave his country ; affirming that it was written, "Abide in the land and support thyself honestly." I knew it was thus translated in German, and found out no better until I came to this country. The first thing I bought, as to reading matter, was an English Bible and a German-English dictionary. Then I soon found out the difference, and I accepted then and do now the English text as the true meaning of the

Holy Spirit. The words are recorded in the 37th
Psalm, 3d verse, " Trust in the Lord and do good,
so shalt thou dwell in the land, and verily thou
shalt be fed."

I went to see my brother in Christ with whom I
first had become acquainted, and whom I regarded
as a man taught of God and an able expounder of
truth.   As soon as I had called his attention to it, he
opened the Bible and pointed to a passage of Scripture, saying, " Thus sayeth the Lord, ' When they persecute you in this city, flee ye into another.' "   This
was good tidings to me, and was exceeding glad
when these precious words of the Lord Jesus were
by his Spirit applied to my heart, as though they
were spoken to me individually.   It was not long
till I was again apprehended by some of the pious
freewillers.   " We have heard that you are fixing to
go to America; you had better be careful.   You
cannot go thither without violating the commandment which says, ' Abide in the land, and support
thyself honestly.' "   I replied : " Again it is written,
' But when they persecute you in this city, flee ye
into another."   This worked like a charm.   All departed in silence, and I was approached upon that
subject no more.   About that time we had received
orders from the company whose ships were on the
ocean back and forth, that we were wanted to take
ship sometime (I think) in May, 1854.   But another
difficulty presented itself in my way.   I had not quite

done with my military duties. And to steal myself
away from the service of my country was what I
abhorred ; consequently, I wrote to my captain, and
told him all, imploring him in the mean time to
forgive me the one year of my reserve duties, as it
had now become impossible for me to stay, the prep-
aration to get off having all been made. The captain answered immediately, that it was not in his
power to allow me the whole twelve months, but
owing to my good behavior in actual service, he
could and would forgive me six months, and no
more. I went to the Chief Justice (Oberammtmann)
of my birth place, where also I then resided, and
told him all from beginning to end.

The Chief Justice was very kind to me and exceedingly accommodating. He gave me papers to
travel with ; I might go where I wished to go, except to Switzerland and America. This would have
been all right for me, had not the under officer,
who had to countersign the papers, put in plain letters his own authority there in the following words ;
"Possessor of these papers is a soldier." Of course
this ruined all. If called upon to show them away
from home, any police officer (Gend-arm) might
have sent me back to my native town. So we burned
the papers, and were ready to depart without any.
Father advised me to wear a coat he had made for
me, with some extra lining and padding inside,

which would not, while I was wearing it, make me look much like a soldier.

Now the day drew near when we must depart and bid adieu to the place of my birth, childhood and youth forever, and to say farewell to all my kindred and friends, leaving them all in the hand of that God who cares for sparrows and hears the cry of ravens. And meantime we thought we had already overcome every obstacle so far, and were looking ahead with a kind of cheerfulness, when the last grievous trouble befell us, which came well nigh breaking old nature's heart. We could not raise the money for the passage of our now three-year old baby. Our furniture would not sell, and besides I had rented a house I yet never lived in, but I had that house rented for one year, before we knew we were ever going to America. Father held us to the rent, and he said we better leave the child with them, ('tis true, poor dears, they loved the babe) he feared the little one might be an incumbrance to us, we both might have to work at the trade; and if we made and saved any money, we might send it and he would then send the child. But oh, how could we leave the little boy behind! I begged father not to be so severe on us, but he insisted and declared it would be better for all concerned. O how could I tell the child's mother? I told it weeping, and her great grief was most distressing to me. As soon as I could find a place by myself I fell on my face,

tried to pray to the Lord but could not. I groaned
at his Majesty's feet till I was weary with groaning.
We had to leave the child behind, the parting hour
drew near, and to describe how I then felt I beg to
omit. I took the little one in my arms, silent tears
rolling down my cheeks, and I kissed the lovely
child till our time was up. A hasty farewell to
grandmother, mother, brothers, and sister, and I was
off. I had concluded to walk an hour or so ahead
of the omnibus which was to carry father and wife
till they overtook me. My purpose in this was that
I might be entirely by myself and alone with my
God.

When I arrived at about a quarter of a mile from
the town, I looked upon the place where I was born
both naturally and spiritually—the town that held
my child under some pretence or other—I leaned
for awhile on the cane or stick I was carrying, and
with the last gaze upon the old place, I said: "Farewell, thou place of my childhood and youth, I shall
never see thee any more. Farewell, ye people who
have loved me, and ye who have been offended at
my following Jesus. You have done it ignorantly,
I verily believe, and may God forgive you and
shower his blessings upon you all. Farewell, grandmother, father, mother, brothers and sister, farewell.
I shall never see you any more. I pray God to bless
you all for Jesus' sake. Fare thee well, my darling
babe. Fare thee well for the present. I have ob-

tained the promise of Jehovah that I shall see thee
again in America, the land whither thy poor parents
are now hastening." The tears now flowed freely,
and with the flow of tears came the sweet words:
"They that sow in tears shall reap in joy." I thought
some one had spoken, when again some one, as it
sounded to me, said: "It is the Lord." Then I
began to sing a song of praise to the dear Redeemer,
and tried to still my tears, when the omnibus came
along that carried my father and my wife, to carry us
two to the ship which was to take us off from the
land I loved, to a land then unknown to all of us.
We had to wait ten days for the ship at Bremerhaven.
At last the day came, when we were ordered on board
the ship. Two policemen came along, and inquired
for a deserter. I supposed they meant me, and I got
awfully scared. My wife said: "Don't scare so; you
look as white as the wall. They are not looking for
you;" and then I heard it was not my name they
called out. I breathed freely once more. That
same hour we sailed, and with a last farewell-sigh,
we left the shores of old fatherland forever.

PART II.

MY EXPERIENCE IN AMERICA.

CHAPTER I.

We sailed from Europe, (Bremerhaven) in June and arrived in America (New York) in August, 1854. We were on the ocean seven weeks in a sail-ship. Some two hundred emigrants, besides crew and officers, were aboard. Religionists of all kinds were there, Tom Payne Infidels, Catholics, Protestants and Jews; but Baptists or believers in the Lord Jesus Christ I found none. Of God and his Christ I never heard a word except in mockery. Oh the loving kindness as well as the long suffering of God ! How unsearchable are his judgments and his ways past finding out! I soon found that I was a speckled bird among all of them. In order to be as much by myself as possible, I sought out and found a place on deck where I could sit down and work at my trade. Thus I set up a kind of tailor shop on the deck of

the ship and immediately got as much as I could
do. My companion being sea-sick, more or less
during the entire voyage, tried nevertheless to be
with me on deck. I was not sea-sick at all, and
hence was able to work ; this made the time pass off
more rapidly to me. The captain we sailed with
was the only one among the officers and crew who
could speak our (the German) language. One time
we had a violent storm which threatened our destruction ; several sails were torn in pieces, the ship was
tossed from side to side for sometime, the waves
rolled over it, thunder and lightning accompanying
the violent winds for awhile, and many of the emigrants were calling each upon their god. At last
the storm ceased and there was a calm, and the
pleasant air invited us all on deck again. The Lord
had spared us, and we perished not. At another
time fire broke out in the night. Great was the
confusion among the poor penned-up emigrants,
and we all feared we were now to perish in a dreadful manner. But a few skillful men succeeded in
extinguishing the flames, and we were saved. Some-
how or other I had at that time been sinking in a
state of carnal ease, and hence was not at all fright-
ened or uneasy as to what might become of us. I
felt no goings out to God. Had I forgotten the rock
of my salvation ? Did I examine myself whether I
was in the faith ? Alas, I did not. A season of darkness had come upon me and I was not conscious of

it. No panting after the living God, and hence, as I verily believe, no manifestation of his loving kindness towards me. No striving to enter into the feelings of Jesus Christ, when he sweat great drops of blood for me. No *feeling* of being shut up, no realizing evidence of my having sunk in the miry clay of carnal sloth and carnal-mindedness; verily, "rottenness had entered into my bones, and I knew it not." I did not feel the plague of sin, that old nature in me, that is as a cage of unclean and hateful birds. And not until we arrived at New York was I made to tremble, to groan and to stagger under it. Then I awoke as out of a deep sleep. The forty-ninth day of our voyage brought us safely to that city. Early in the morning of that day we heard the watchman on deck call out the long desired call; "Land! Land!" We all went on deck, and, O, wonder, what a glorious sight to behold! I remarked: "If the sight of land in this world after a long voyage on water is so beautiful, what must it be in yonder regions where no sin is, nor sinful beings can ever come?" ·Now we spent the time in looking and admiring at the landscape as we passed slowly along. Oh why had I not a tear of gratitude or a song of praise at that time? Lord, forgive thy poor worm; I have received thy blessings all my lifetime and have been ungrateful in return!

In the afternoon we were told to go ashore. In New York I was to send a telegraphic dispatch to

4

Cincinnati for means to go to that city. When on my way there I met one on the street who had served in the army with me, and who was one of the leaders of the little band of worshippers I mentioned in another place. His name was Plaatye. He had not united with the Grace Baptists, but had gone over to the other side. He and his wife both received us very kindly and invited us to stay with them until we should get the money to depart for Cincinnati. I had done some work for some of the crew on board of the ship, and had to wait there three or four days till they were paid off. Now I disliked sending a dispatch to my brother asking him for more money, and we chose rather to sell some of our clothing, jewelry, etc. We sold all and lacked ten dollars still. I was at my wit's end. I knew not what to do. To send a dispatch to Cincinnati now and then wait for the arrival of the money seemed to take up too much time; and our friend, who also was a tailor, and one of the poor of this world's goods, could not well keep us any longer, (though he did not say so,) for I saw he could get no more work for us to do. Both my wife and myself had been working for him in order to pay for our board, but work had now given out. The dullest season of the year had just then began. To stay in New York until work commenced again would not do, because I was in debt to my brother, and he looked for us to come to Cincinnati. To sell more of our stuff would

not do, because we had nothing that would bring
as much as ten dollars except a bed which we were
unwilling to give up. But rather than ask John for
any more money, we determined to sell it also, if the
Lord did not help. The very thought of the Lord's
help brought me to my senses again. I looked up
to him; but oh, where had I been? I felt ashamed,
convicted and condemned. Wandering in sin's dark
maze, I had not so much as thought upon His
name,—to ask Him to deliver me from all evil, to
shield me from all harm, and to conduct me safe to
the place he had directed me to. I could but make
my complaints known by groanings which cannot
be uttered. I begged the Lord to help me. " Whom
have I in heaven but thee, and there is none on
earth that I should desire besides thee." O Lord,
do show me a token for good, deliver me out of this
great distress. I was out on the streets of New York
when sending this poor petition to the throne of
God. Returning to the house I found my wife conversing with our friends on the same subject, and all
they and I could say was that we knew not what to
do. At that very moment a man stepped into the
house who was a brother in the faith to my friend.
This man told my friend that he had received a letter from some one in Chicago requesting him to let
a certain man, who was to arrive from Germany in
such a ship—naming the one on which we came—
have ten dollars. He had been searching for him,

but though the vessel was in port, he could not find
his man. Now the man he spoke of I knew well,
and I had also seen him go off on the cars for Chicago. Ilis name was Wrede. I told the gentleman
so, and he concluded that his accommodation was
not needed in this case. My friend told him who I
was and in what circumstances I was placed; when
he remarked immediately that he knew my father
well, and with the greatest pleasure would he let me
have the money if I would accept it. Had I not
been so hard-hearted I should have burst into a flood
of grateful tears to my God. Gladly I accepted his
offer, told him this was the Lord's directions, and
forthwith we took the train for Cincinnati.

CHAPTER II.

It was in August, 1854, about one year subsequent
to my baptism when we arrived safely at the city of
Cincinnati. Found my brother at his boarding
house in good health. As soon as he saw us, he
looked around, amazed not to see our child with us.
When we told him the circumstances he became in-
dignant, and wrote immediately to our parents de-
nouncing their hard measures and cruel treatment;
but I could not and would not give my consent to it.
On hearing my story about the money borrowed

in New York, my brother smiled and immediately sent the ten dollars back to the man, with many thanks; he answered that he received it all right, and that was the last I ever heard of him. His name was Boon. May the Lord remember their labor of love.

I was in hopes of finding a believer in my brother John,—but in this I was disappointed. He had turned an infidel, and told me forthwith that he believed nothing, and I should have to drop the humbug of religion, because here in America every one was in for making money. I felt exceedingly sorry for him, and was constrained to acknowledge and say: Oh, Lord, wonderful are thy ways! Thou canst and dost make use of infidels to deliver one of thy humble poor from oppression, and bring him to a country where persecution on account of one's religious sentiments is not tolerated. Yea, verily, men and devils are under the control of Almighty God.

My brother had rented a room for us and furnished the same with the necessary furniture. One bedstead, two chairs, a small table and a broom composed the whole of it. A little furnace served for heating a tailor's goose and to cook by. The bedstead is in our possession yet. With the furnace we only lately parted. My brother had also suc-ceeded in obtaining work for me, and for the first time in my life I went to a clothing store to receive the work. I was astonished when I heard the cutter tell me, they only paid one dollar and twenty-five cents for the making of heavy winter coats—all to be made by hand. The thought, how shall I pay my brother, was almost uppermost in my mind, and more so now, when I found that with such wages I could scarcely make a living, unless I had always steady work. However, I took the first bundle of coats on my shoulder and carried them to our room, which was about ten or twelve squares from the store. On my way home I got into a dreadful state of rebellion. I thought about Weener—my native town in Germany. There, before I joined the Baptists, I had a good business of my own, which I had obtained with (to me) great cost and eleven years of labor; had a fine start, and good prospects for the future. Then I had my journeymen and apprentices, and every convenience to be desired. Oh, the flesh-pots of Egypt!

Now, I was deep in debt, having no means to pay with, my child thousands of miles away, myself carrying a bundle of clothes almost too heavy for my strength, my wife waiting with anxiety for my return ; and after all, no prospect of making a decent living, and but little hope of ever seeing the child again. With heaviness in the heart, which made it stoop, I went home with my great bundle. I threw it down, opened it, and having no table to work on, sat down on the floor, and in this way made up the

coats, all by hand. My wife had never worked on
men's clothes before, but she learned it now, and
she scarcely could find time to cook a little coffee, in
which we dipped our dry bread morning and evening. At noon we cooked soup, and someties a few
potatoes, and once a week perhaps a little meat.
When my brother found out that we worked so hard
and lived on so little, he would not have it so. He
wanted us to eat and drink as we used to do in fatherland, if he never got a cent of his money back.
But we would not do it; we worked night and day,
with as little sleep as possible, and of the first
month's work we realized twelve dollars over and
above all expenses. I offered the money to my
brother, but he would not take it; he said there
were better times coming, and then we might think
of paying him. But instead of better times, our
work in that store gave out, and I went in search of
another shop. I succeeded in finding some more
work, and was told if I were willing to make boys'
(youths') coats at thirty-seven and a half cents a
piece, I might take a bundle. I cannot describe the
desperate feeling I now had. What was I to do?
I knew not the English language—I understood
only yes and no—or else I should have gone to some
merchant-tailoring establishment for work, where
prices were better than in the wholesale shops. I
was ignorant of the fact that almost all the mer-

chant tailors who were not themselves Germans kept German cutters, clerks, journeymen, &c.

When I was on the street with my half a dozen thirty-seven and a half cent coats, I wished I had never been born. O what shall I do? The Lord will surely slay me now with famine. I had thoughts of destroying myself, and Satan said, " It is all over with you now. Better drown yourself, you will never be able to pay your brother and how will you get your child." But I then remembered that Satan is a liar and a murderer from the beginning. I remembered that my brother had already sent on the money for the little boy and for some one to bring him. Thus I staggered home like a drunken man, though I did not use strong drink then. But we went to work, and by the time we had our coats done, work had stopped entirely, and now I thought all was lost. I tried to get something to do, no difference what; though I did not know how to work at anything but my trade, yet even in this I did not succeed. I was nigh unto despair, though my brother would let us have what we wanted. I saw I was sinking deeper and deeper in his debt, and one morning early, I concluded by myself, I would put an end to my existence, and went with a full determination to do so. When I came to the canal, I thought maybe some one may see me, I will not drown myself, I will run away, and no one shall hear of me any more. However, with these desperate feelings, I stepped into a merchant tailor shop and introduced myself as a tailor, when the man began to talk German to me. This surprised me, and I took courage to tell the gentleman the condition I was in. He said I could have work if I would make vests, he would give one dollar a piece for making. I gladly accepted the offer, ran home and told my wife about the good fortune, but I never told her what my feelings had been previous to this. When the vest was done, I carried it to him, and he said I was a good vest maker, I could have work as long as he had any.

Now, you see, dear reader, that I had sunk exceedingly low, just ready to give up, yet in the midst of feelings like the above, I had a strong desire to find a spiritual companion. I thought if could find one who loved the Lord Jesus Christ in sincerity, then I would not feel so desperate any more. Oh that I could find one that understood me and my feelings, one that could sympathize with me. And thou, O my precious Lord, was to me, at a distance, yet so near, and I knew it not.

Though His providence seemed to be against me, though I was for a time (apparently at least) delivered to the buffetings of Satan, and my soul was bowed down within me—yet my gracious Lord did not leave me altogether. Sometime the hope of eventually finding some one or more, who were exercised in some manner like myself, would come in

my mind.   Yet if not—the Lord himself had again
and again assured me in my heart that *himself*
would be for a little sanctuary to his sinful and
unprofitable worm.   My Lord kept up the desire to
find believing Baptists also, in my mind—even in
the midst of tossings to and fro, which I had keenly
felt in providence.

———

CHAPTER III.

One Sunday morning I went in search of the
people of God.   The first Sunday after my first
week's work, I started out to find Baptists.   I labored
under the impression that the Lord's people in this
country were situated, to some extent at least, like
they were in Germany; namely, a few gathered together perhaps in some insignificant looking house,
and as I went through many streets I was all the
time listening, if peradventure I might hear some
few singing one of the songs of Zion; then I would
go and join in with them.   But I did not get to hear
the joyful sound.   Now I had been told that on
ninth street there was a Baptist church, and surely,
thought I, I cannot help finding it.   Accordingly, I
went the whole length of that street in search of the
Baptist church three times that Sunday morning,
and when I was about giving up of ever finding it,

I ventured to ask some man who came out of a large, fine meeting house they called church, if he knew where the Baptist church might be. He smiled and pointed to the large building, and said, "There it is." I did not know what to think of it, but I thought he had not told me the truth, and I did not go in. Several little children met me next, and I inquired of them, and one little girl pointed out the same large building, and said: "There is the Baptist Church." I said to myself, can it be possible? O Lord, whither have thy people come to in this country? I went into the magnificent building and beheld a fine carpet on the floor, and I could not believe that that was a place where Baptists worshipped. Oh, I thought, if my parents were to see this, they would begin to think that Baptists were respectable indeed. However, I stepped in, and with much hesitation, I ventured to go into one of the velvet-cushioned pews and set down, waiting to see what would come next. The people, richly clad, gathered in, and at last one man stepped into the pulpit who did not look to me like a preacher; he wore a mustache. I thought he could not be a preacher, for I had never seen a preacher wearing a mustache. However, he took the book, read a chapter, and then fingered out of his breast-pocket a little pamphlet, which I took to be his sermon, and put it in the Bible which lay open before him. Now he began to read his first prayer. Of course I could not under-

stand the language, but I could see him read, and
when he began to read, the people leaned forward a
little bit, and the ladies held their fans to their fore-
heads, from all of which I concluded it was the form
of a prayer he was reading. Then he took a little
book and read (as I thought) a hymn, and immediately after the reading, a band of fiddlers began to
play. These I had not noticed before, because they
were seated in the gallery right back of me. I took
my hat and ran out as quick as I could, fully persuaded in my own mind that the name " *Baptist*" in
this country did not always mean what it meant in
Germany. Where I came from, the name " *Baptist*"
was identical with the offscouring of all things, the
despised, the ones hated of all men for the truth's
sake, identical with the ones destitute of worldly
ease, grandeur and applause, tormented with in-
dwelling sin, afflicted because they cannot cease
from sin, while here it seemed to be just the reverse.
My hope of finding Baptists that day was dashed to
shivers, and as the poet says:

> "I to my own sad place returned,
>   My loneliness to feel:
> I sigh—I pant—I grieve and mourn,
>   And am but barren still."

The following Sunday I went in another direction
in search of Baptists. Having learned that there
were some " Holland Baptists " in Cincinnati over
the canal, I started in search of them, and was not

long in finding a little, humble-looking building
which they called the "Holland Baptist Church."
Upon inquiry I was informed that as soon as the
Sunday School was over, the meeting would begin.
When the school was out the children seemed to
be glad, for they stormed out of the house with a
great noise. Now I went in, and as I could speak
and understand the Holland language, as well as
the German, I helped them sing, and when the
preacher began speaking, I was all attention. His
text was Cant. 4: 16, "Awake, O north wind, and
come thou south; blow upon my garden that the
spices thereof may flow out. Let my beloved come
into his garden and eat his pleasant fruit." All the
while he was preaching I remembered having read
the sermon before. It seemed so near like Krummacher's sermon upon the same text, that it was not
new to me, neither did I find anything in it that did
my wounded, sin smitten soul any good. After
preaching, the minister asked me who I was, just
fresh from the fatherland, and where I now lived
in the city, and voluntarily promised to come and
see me, which he accordingly did, accompanied by
two of his brethren. Now they began to ask many
questions about the Baptists in Germany, which I
answered as well as I could, and then the preacher
asked me if I had a letter. I had not so much as
heard of such a thing before, and hence I told him
the Free Grace Baptists in Germany held that "we

need not, as some others, epistles of commendation
to you or letters of commendation from you," and
while I said this, the preacher stretched his face I
don't know how long. I got somewhat afraid of
him. I though he had gone crazy, for with a long
and loud O o-o-o-h, he ran out of the house and his
brethren followed him in silence, and I saw them
no more to this day.

Now I gave up all hopes of finding any one in
that great city that feared God, and my distress
greatly increased. I groaned and wept sometime,
so that I was sick and wearied with groanings that
cannot be uttered, and my eyes pained me with
weeping. Oh for a place on earth where I could be
by myself. Everything and every one in this large
city seemed to be against me. I cried to God, but
he heard not; to the Most High I brought my complaints, but he gave me no answer. Dear children
of God, if any of you have been similarly tried you,
can understand what I am talking about.

Five months we had now been in Cincinnati, and
had not been able to pay off one cent of our great
debt. Look which way I would I saw no help. I
was hedged in on all sides with nothing but rebellion and sin in my heart. But, oh, blessed be his
dear and most precious name, the Lord soon broke
the snare asunder! He sent deliverance to the poor
captive. He appeared in loving kindness and light,
life and liberty were abundantly enjoyed for a long

season. The Lord had triumphed gloriously. All opposing elements, the horse and his rider had he thrown into the sea! Praise the Lord, O my soul, and all that is within me bless his holy name forever and ever. Amen.

CHAPTER IV.

One morning I had obtained a little work again; but at the same time I felt so down-hearted, distressed and forlorn, that while I was at work, I could not refrain from weeping. My heart was full to overflowing. I managed, however, to hide my tears from my companion. Now all at once it came to my mind how often the Psalms of David had given me unspeakable consolation in times of grief and distress, and involuntarily I took up the Bible once more and turned to the 42d Psalm. When I came to the last verse I could hold to myself no longer, my tears of distress were in an instant changed to tears of joy and gladness, and I breathed out crying, saying: "Oh Lord, art thou still my Lord and my God?" The last two words of the Psalm, "my God" overwhelmed me completely, I saw myself once more sitting at Jesus' feet, clothed and in my right mind. I told my wife not to despair now, I said "all is well, all is well. The Lord hath done all

things well! I was sure that the Lord would soon
appear for us, and that gloriously!" While I was
yet speaking with fullness of joy and much assurance, some one knocked at the door. I arose and
opened the door and two men came in the room: one
was a stranger to me, but the other one was the mer-
chant-tailor who had given me work occasionally.
He spoke in English to the stranger and pointed to
me; then he addressed me in German, and said:
" Mr. Greenwood, this gentlemen wants a cutter, and
foreman for his business, and because I know you
would suit him, I thought of recommending you.
You are to go with him for one week, then if you
both can agree, he will give you good wages."

I thought he wanted me at once. I pulled off my
old working habit and said: " Of course I will go.
Must I go now?" They smiled perhaps at my sim-
plicity, but oh had they known the emotions of my
heart, and my longing desire for just such a situation coming to me just at the time when a visitation
from on high had favored me and changed my night
to day; yet they were very kind to me and said:
" No, to-morrow at two o'clock will do." I was to go
with him in the country some thirty-three miles to
a place called Clover, Clermont county. And they
departed. I called them back, however, and told
them I had forgotten to inform them that I could
not as yet talk English. The interpreter then said
to me, " The gentleman don't care whether you talk

English or not, he said he hired you to work and
not to talk." Oh the delight of my soul; just as my
precious Lord had promised. All turned out well.
The very words " in the country," sounded like
sweet music in my ears. Just what I had desired of
my Lord. As soon as the men had departed I wept
aloud for joy and gratitude to my God, and my dear
tried wife wept too; yea I wept and danced and rejoiced before the Lord all at the same time. Oh my
soul, bow at his footstool low, bow the chief of sinners at my Saviour's feet. Then came in my brother
who was astonished to see me thus. A few words to
him explained all, and he went and bought me a
pair of fine boots and made me a present of them.
Oh what a long time appeared those twenty-four
hours while waiting to see my future employer again.
We reasoned, suppose the man backs out? I said,
no, he cannot back out; this thing is of the Lord, and
the Lord's work is perfect. But perhaps I might not
suit the man. The Lord will make me suit him. I
know he will. O thou faith, thou substance of
things hoped for, thou evidence of things not seen.
By this precious gift of God I was as confident and
as sure of it as I was of my own existence. The
whole night almost was spent in fixing up somewhat
decently. At last the time came and I went, overwhelmed with happiness and joy to the place he had
designated, and after two hours' delay we got in the

stage at last. Now I found that there also was a journeyman tailor with us, who was to serve as interpreter. Mr. Hitch, for this was the gentleman's name, talked to me in the stage, but alas! not a word could I understand. When he saw it distressed me he patted me on the shoulder and told me by the interpreter to never mind, we would get to understand one another by and by. At last we arrived at Clover, the place of our destination. I could then make melody in my heart and felt like singing: "Blessed be the Lord God who only doeth wondrous things, and blessed be his glorious name forever, and let the whole earth be filled with his glory." Psalms 72: 18, 19. I could indeed hold sweet communion with my dearest Lord, and my precious Lord did then and there give me a grateful heart. I was enabled to sing songs of praise to his dear name for his exceeding great and precious promises, which then came home to me, as though they all were mine, and had always been my very own. Brethren, beloved of the Lord, gracious and believing reader, suffer once more a little word of exhortation. What is all religion without communion with the blessed Saviour? I want to hear his sweet voice daily. I want him to speak to me occasionally that all is well between my soul and my God. What I want is reality. I want to feel that I, even I myself, have an interest in Jesus and his love merely to read in his word that Christ came into the world to save sinners, even the chief of them, is not enough for me.

> Election 'tis a precious truth,
> No comfort there I see,
> Till I am told by God's own mouth
> That he hath chosen me.

Even the letter of Scripture itself is insufficient to convince me of this fact; nay, verily, unless Jehovah Himself, God the Holy Ghost, is graciously pleased to proclaim the glad tidings to my soul, I am almost ready to sink in despair. Talk of creature goodness, creature efforts, creature religion, creature piety, creature duties, &c., to one who is altogether as an unclean thing, who, like the children of Israel, knows no way of escape from guilt, tossed to and fro like the dawning of the day, sometimes perplexed, distressed, troubled on all sides; never able to forget the wormwood and the gall of past offences, a groaning, sighing, weeping individual, never satisfied until the Lord appears with His living, soul-cheering word, saying: "Fear not, I have redeemed thee, thou art mine." Then I can draw living water out of the well of salvation. And oh! if but a glimpse of Jesus is obtained, how lovely, how consoling, how cheering, how endearing, how precious, does the poor sinner's best friend then appear! but not until Jesus does appear do I find peace. God's dear people are tried people, and none but the Lord God Almighty can give them rest. Oh for

grace to sit at Jesus' feet weeping, and in my feelings bathe his dear feet with my tears, until he speak
the word to worthless me, saying: "Be of good cheer,
it is I. I have loved thee with an everlasting love ;
therefore, with loving kindness I have drawn thee.
I, even I, have blotted out thy transgressions for mine
own sake, and thy sins and thy iniquities will I remember no more."

Oh, my father's children, I want to live upon Jesus Christ as the bread of life. I want to eat his
flesh and drink his blood! I want him to clothe me
with the garments of salvation, all other clothing to
me—such as I can make not exempted—are but
dried up fig leaves at best. I want Jesus to cover
me with the robe of righteousness. I want to have
within me "faith"—the faith of the Son of God,
which is not dead—but living faith, the faith of
God's elect, the faith once delivered to the saints.
This faith is more than notion, it allows none to be
at ease in Zion, it keeps us active and enables us to
give all diligence to make our calling and election
sure. It works by love, and is infinitely more than
a great deal of studied divinity in the head. It works
in the heart, the seat of our affections, and tells us
that

> "A form of words, howe'er so sound,
>   Can never save a soul:
> The Holy Ghost must give the wound,
>   And make the wounded whole."

CHAPTER V.

The beloved reader who has followed me patiently so far, will bear with me a little longer while I may try to describe my feelings under the banner of love, where my precious Saviour had sweetly brought me in his banqueting house, and he kept up his love-visits to the time when he was pleased to give me up my little boy safe and sound, which was over two years and a half. The dear Lord was graciously pleased to keep up in my once overburdened, but now gratefully overflowing heart, a constant flow of living love. I felt aften ready to exclaim aloud, " The air is perfumed with his breath." With feelings of constant praise to God, my eyes often over-flowing with tears, I could but gaze, wonder and adore the unspeakable love of the Lord Jesus Christ! And that to such a poor moth as I am! O how I felt the sweet words of the poet when he, in speaking of Christ, seems to sing with pleasing admiration and praise :

> Love sits in his eyelids and scatters delight,
> Through all the bright mansions on high ;
> Their faces the cherubim veil in his sight,
> And tremble with fullness of joy.

Yes, beloved reader, I did feel then and there that the morning or day star had arisen in my heart, and have often been enabled with rapture to exclaim in his ears alone :

> He is *my* bright and morning star,
> I see his glories from afar,
> I *know* the glorious morning star.

Thus was my blessed Lord graciously pleased to give me that faith that worketh by his own sweet love, and I realized that without that living faith it is impossible to please God. Moreover I learned also that without this living faith which must flow from God, I am but barren, careless, worldly-minded, unconcerned and dead; however alive to sin I may be, thirsting for fame, for wealth or a good name. Oh blessed Jesus, my adorable Saviour, my Lord and my God! Do thou be pleased to shed forth the grace of faith into the hearts of thine own dear children. How can Thy poor ask of God wisdom and instruction, without thy Holy Spirit? How can they know as to how they should walk in this world and behave in thy house without thy love-visits, the outpouring of thy Holy Spirit in their heart? Oh do, dear Lord, impart this living faith in our, by sin, downtrodden souls, and quicken us according to thy word! May thy dear children be enabled to more perfectly and earnestly contend for the faith *once* delivered to the saints, viz: vital and experimental godliness. Whence comes the emptiness and barrenness of many professors? Whence comes so much presumption and self-confidence? Are you

not really tried and exercised in your souls? Are
you acquainted with your own helplessness? Are
you not really in trouble as other men (the prophets)
or plagued like other men (the apostles)? For my
part I can inform my Father's children that I want
to discover in myself, as well as in others, the works
and evidences of eternal life. And flesh and blood
cannot reveal this to us. I want fervency in prayer,
brokenness of heart and contrition of spirit. I want
to strive against sin. I want much speaking one to
another of the dealings of the Lord with our souls.
I want solicitude with my brethren in regard to our
state. Hence, I want the *unction*, power, savour or
heavenly dew *from on high;* and whereas I find myself most of my time destitute of all this, I am most
of my time groaning, sighing and crying to my God,
until he is pleased to lift upon me the light of his
countenance. Then I feel the leprosy of sin, then I
feel my need of Christ, and cry, "Jesus, thou son of
David, have mercy on me." And when I am healed
and have a thankful heart given me, then I can
glorify God. But alas! how soon do I forget the
loving kindness of the Lord. Night comes suddenly
upon me, and I stumble—falling among thieves—
worldly lust, worldly cares, worldly greed of filthy
lucre and a thousand more of things that savor
of the flesh only—I suppose to rise no more! But,
lo! here comes the good Samaritan, and bless
his lovely name, ere I am aware, he has raised me

up again, and is pouring the oil of gladness in my wounded heart, and the wine of his eternal love in my lips. Then I lisp his praises and speak of his tender mercies. Again, I am forgetful of my best friend, that sticketh closer than an earthly brother. Satan takes the advantage and buffets me with hard thoughts of God, and gradually I see myself sunk so low that I am compelled to conclude: Surely now I am ruined. I have fallen by the hand of my enemy. Now I sigh and pant, groan, pray, weep and mourn, but all to no purpose. It seems sometimes that my heart would break for sorrow. O wretched man that I am! I am like a painted sepulchre. The brethren think you are a saint, says Satan, but if they only knew that God would not hear your prayers, surely they would cast you off and own you no more forever. Then I would fain creep into the earth could I but do so. Oh that I had wings like a dove, then I would fly away at be at rest. Then with indescribable anguish I cry : "God be merciful to me, a sinner! Lord, save! Lord, help! I perish!" and ere I am aware of it, a gentle, sweet whisper of indescribable peace is wafted in my troubled soul; I feel like as if mercy has taken hold of my heart, the name of Jesus at once becomes very precious once more, and I sing, "Victory, victory, through the blood of the Lamb!"

But to return. I will now try to relate what pleasant seasons I have experienced in the glorious deliverance God had wrought for me, independent of men, for as yet I knew no living man in this great country who might have conversed with me about the heavenly land, the fruit to eat thereof is life eternal.

When the Lord had brought me out of Cincinnati to the above named place (Clover), then I did enjoy the privilege of communing with the Saviour from off his mercy seat. Arriving at the house of my employer, I was introduced as the new cutter, and after supper we were shown to our room. Such a flood of light, life, liberty, peace and comfort as burst upon my enraptured soul that night I shall never forget. And I verily thought with the sweet singer of Israel: "While I live I will praise the Lord. I will sing praises unto my God while I have my being. Happy is he that hath the God of Jacob for his help, whose help is in the Lord his God, * * which executeth judgment for the oppressed, which giveth food to the hungry. The Lord looseth the prisoners. He hath not dealt so with any nation, and as for his judgments, they have not known them. Praise ye the Lord."

The next morning we were shown to a little tailor shop standing entirely by itself across the road, and to work we went forthwith. The first trial work I had to do here was cutting and making a coat for a man who was a tailor himself, but had quit the business. While I was making the coat the man who

5

served as interpreter was also working in the same shop with me, and he, being an infidel, frequently would remark that he believed that I was either crazy or homesick, for I would not talk to him much, and if he ask me about anything, I would often give him wrong answers. Sometimes, said he, he observed me weeping like a child, then again I would appear to be as happy as one could be. He said he could not tell what was the matter with me. Poor soul, he knew not anything of this matter; this was between David and Jonathan alone.

Thus time passed on until I had my coat done. My employer came into the shop and tried it on himself, and, as talking to himself, I understood him to say: "About right, about right." I took my German-English Dictionary and found what the "about" meant, when my heart became full of heaviness. And heaviness in the heart maketh it to stoop. About right, thought I. Why not altogether right? And it made me feel sad for a little while. But this was not to last long. The good word that was to make the stooped heart glad again came speedily. The customer for whom the coat was made came into the shop while my employer was yet there; he tried the coat on himself, and then said, "Splendid, indeed!" and both left the shop. Dictionary again helped me out, and I was not long in finding what the word "splendid" meant, and it welled up in my heart somewhat in this wise: "Oh, Lord, if this man

was not working with me here, I would sing so loud
that heaven and earth might hear. But man or no
man, I began to sing the old Holland Psalmody:
" Bless the Lord, O my soul, and all that is within
me bless his holy name," &c., and the journeyman
said I was the strangest man he had ever seen.

Beloved, let me give here the first verse of that
precious Psalm, as I then sang it. Psalm 103 : 1, 2 :

> Loof, loof then Heer myn
> Ziel met alle krachten
> Verhef zyn naam zoo groot zoo heilig t'achten.
> Och! of nu all what in my ishem prees';
> Loof, loof myn ziel then hoorder der gebeden
> Vergeet nooit een van zyn weldadigheden
> Vergeet ze niet, t'is God die z'u bewees.

My heart was filled with thankfulness and my
lips with thanksgiving. I tried to be by myself
where I might give vent to my feelings before the
Lord. Seeing I could not at that time neither talk
nor sing in English, another beautiful hymn (German) came, among a great many others, to refresh
my longing soul, which was then so anxious to mag-
nify the Lord in a song of praise. Here it is :

> Kœnut' auch eine Mutter dessen
> Den sie im Shoosse trug vergessen
> Der Herr vergisst doch deiner nicht,
> Wenn dich Seine Hand nicht fuehrte,
> Sein Geist nicht deinen Geist regierte,
> Mit Seinem heil'gen Recht und Licht,
> Ach ohne Trost und Rath

Verloorst du Weg und Pfad
   Hallelujah!
Sein Angesicht
Bleibt unser Licht
Wenn aller Welten Bau Zerbricht ! !

Which being interpreted is nearly as follows:

Could a mother forget her offspring?
The Lord will never forget thee.
Did *not* his hand lead thee.
Did *not* his spirit control thy spirit
With his own holy righteousness and light—
Alas! destitute of true comfort and counsel,
Thou must stray from the way of holiness
And the path of truth.
But now—!
   Hallelujah!
His countenance
Remains to be our light.
When worlds upon worlds are crumbling in sunder.

CHAPTER VI.

Thus I learned how graciously the dear Lord was
pleased to bless my labors there, and when I had
worked one week, I found out to my surprise, that
my fellow workman, the interpreter, was discharged,
and the man left the same day. Now I was entirely
by myself. None could understand my language,
nor could I understand any one, because, as far as I

knew, there were no Germans living in the place.
Had I not known most assuredly that the Lord Jesus
Christ understood me altogether, I should not have
stayed. But of that I was sure, and that was enough
for me. However, I tried to ask my employer in
some way whether he meant to discharge me too,
" No," said he, " You must stay. I paid my other
cutter twenty-five dollars a month, I will pay you
thirty dollars, furnish you a house free of rent to
live in and keep you in fire wood all the year; besides, I will move you and wife and household stuff,
free of charge from Cincinnati." When he left I
locked the door and then broke out in a flood of
silent tears of gratitude to my Heavenly Father, saying: "Oh Lord, what can I render unto thee, what
can I say or do to praise thy holy name for so great
manifestations of loving kindness towards such a
poor worm as I?" I cannot describe the joys I felt.
I saw my way clear now, and would soon be able to
pay off all my debts. And then bright hopes of
seeing our little one again cheered and gladdened
my heart. And then—and then—oh, there was no
end to the prospects of a bright future now before
me. And I cried: "It is enough! Lord it is enough!
I am overwhelmed with thy goodness." Though I
had been there now about two weeks, I noticed that
friendly faces met me all around. I had a good rep-
utation already, round about. I was the happiest
individual (I thought) on earth. The day finally

came when we went for my wife and moveables.
Arriving at home once more, the first word my wife
spoke was: "Are you going to stay?" I replied,
"yes, dear, all is well;" and then we cried awhile for
joy and gratitude. Now I began to tell her all, and
I think this was one of the happiest days we ever
had on earth. Now we fixed for moving, and in a
short time all was fixed to move for our new habi-
tation. "The Lord hath done great things for us,
whereof we are glad." "They that sow in tears shall
reap in joy." Amen and amen.

In my new calling as foreman and cutter, the dear
Lord was pleased to enable me to see his hand in all
my undertakings. He turned my duties into delights, and my daily sacrifices into glorious privi-
leges. I was filled with joy and peace in believing,
and the candle of the Lord shone round about me.
Cheerfully I went to my work, singing praises to my
God with thanksgiving, day after day, for a long
time. On the first Sunday of our living in the place,
I wondered if peradventure there might be some
one somewhere like myself in belief, practice, walk
and conversation. A desire to find a spiritual companion was uppermost in my mind. Of course I
had my wife, but she made *me* her all in all, and
that did not satisfy me ; I wanted one that makes
Christ Jesus, the God of the whole earth, the all in all
needful for time and eternity. Some way I had
found out there were Baptists living in Bethel, a

town about three or four miles from Clover. The name of the town I thought was good, and I concluded I would go and see if, perhaps, I might find a Nazarene. Had I sought the Scriptures upon this point, I might have discovered what I found afterwards, namely that is written: "Seek not Bethel." Amos 5:5. But I did not so search the Scriptures, neither experienced I a certain freedom to ask the Lord to let me find a spiritual relative in that place. On arriving there, however, I found a meeting house with the inscription : "BAPTIST CHURCH." I thought it strange, as I do yet, to call a building of wood or stone by that name, because the word "Church" was then and is now sacred to me. I never had understood it to be anything less or more than "the Body of Christ. The Lamb's wife." "He loved her so without a but, if, or ought. He gave himself for her, that he might sanctify and cleanse her with the washing of water by the word. That he might present her to himself a glorious church, not having spot or wrinkle or any such thing, but that she should be holy and without blemish." Eph. 5:25, 27. I have quoted it here as it is translated in the German translation of the Bible. Still, I thought, may be the inscription, "Baptist Church," may have reference to a body of christians worshipping at that place, and I ventured to go in. I prayed to God that he would be pleased to make it known unto me when any of his dear children entered the building.

I was about the first one who had come in. I kept
constantly watching the door. One by one the people came in, but there was no manifestation. Now
I prayed in my spirit to the living God: "Oh,
Father, if there are indeed any of thy loved ones in
this house, be pleased to make it known to me and
cause them to look friendly at me, or shake hands
with me, or speak a kind word to me, after the service is over." This service consisted in what they
called, (as I afterwards found out) a speaking meeting. One after another arose and said something,
but I could not understand what they were saying.
When it was over, one dismissed the meeting, and
then I placed myself in a position where most of the
folks assembled had to pass me. Not a kind look
did I obtain, not a single one shook hands with me,
neither did any one speak to me at all. Now, I went
back home again with rather an aching heart; but
my precious Lord broke in upon my soul with much
sweetness, and assured me that he was much more
to me than ten companions and that he would be
very near unto me and *draw* me, and I should *run
after him alone.* Yea, the words he spake to me, came
with power and much persuasion, saying, "Am I
not more unto thee than ten brethren?" I said, yea,
Lord, forgive me that I have for a moment forgotten
thee. And he was pleased, bless his dear name forever and ever, he was graciously pleased to go with
me all the way, and though it was a very cold day

(January, 1855) yet my heart burned within me while he was communing with his poor prodigal. When I arrived home once more I told my wife it was useless for me to hunt up Baptists, that is to say, living Baptists, who loved the Lord Jesus Christ as the way, the truth and the life. Yet I kept on in search of them for two years in succession every Sunday, until the memorable year of 1857 greeted me with showers of grace in my heart and manifestations of God's faithfulness in causing me to find his people, and in giving us back our child as it were from the dead. But people would reason with me, and I soon learned enough of the English tongue to carry on a common conversation with people. They would tell me I was too particular, and they did not think there were any in this whole country that I could agree with or they with me. No doubt but what others were as good christians as myself, but I was too hard, would give none a chance, etc. This was poor reasoning to me. But such reasoners did not understand my case. I felt my nothingness continually, and all I wanted was to find one or two that felt their nothingness too. I knew that the world was full of exalted professors of religion, but they stood too high for me. I was poor in my Father's house (poor in spirit) and of low estate too. And my heart's desire was to find another poor one crying to God, hungry and thirsty for the bread of life. I knew the dear Lord sends the rich folks

empty away, but not *until* the same Lord makes
them *feel* their emptiness and poverty, will they beg
for bread.   I wanted to find one like myself, a leper,
a healed leper, whom Jesus had cured of his leprosy,
and who now would gladly return with me and falling down on his face give glory to God.   I wanted
to find a babe who with me would lift up his voice
singing: Hosannah to the Prince of Life for his
wonderful works which he hath done for our once
lost souls!   Oh, yes! I desired to find one who, compelled by sovereign grace and constrained by ever-
'lasting love to press his way through, in order to
touch the hem of Jesus' garment, to obtain healing
from the loathsome pestilence, even the sin of unbelief that so easily besets us.   I wanted the compan-
ionship of one or more who, with me, could sit at
Jesus' feet weeping, and with me sing of his redeeming love!   What is there that is hard about all this?
I could not see anything wrong in it, though the
whole world were to ridicule and treat me with contempt for it.

Now, it came to pass in those days that a portion
of professed christians held a meeting at the meeting-house nearly opposite where I stayed.   I went
to the meeting, and the leaders had been pleased to
make me, or chosen me, to be their Bible-class teacher
for their Sunday School.   I was ignorant of all this,
never having been at such a place before, and I had
no idea that the Bible was used at all to further a

new invention of theirs, they called Sabbath School.
I thought I had to accept, and accepted the new
role. I requested the class to read the 1st chapter
of John's Gospel for the.first Sunday's lesson, which
they might look over during the coming week.
When Sunday next came, there were about twenty
or twenty-two men in the class (young and old), with
every one of whom I was well acquainted, but had
never noticed any of them to possess spiritual or
eternal life. When all had read a verse the questioning began, and, as I had expected, I had to do
the questioning and the answering of my own questions, and not until we came to. the verse: "The
law was given by Moses, but grace and truth came
by Jesus Christ," I showed a determination to elicit
one answer from some one; and, having obtained
an answer, I proved to the class that there was a
difference somewhere, because the Holy Ghost by
Paul declared it to be so and so, And then quoted
some Scripture on the subject. But all at once one
in the class cried out, "If you want to preach such
doctrine, you must go to the Baptists, we here don't
want it." They were Methodists, and of course had
no use for Bible or Baptist doctrine. I shut the
book, and said: "Thank you, sir, and good-day, gentlemen;" and went out of their meeting-house to be
a Sabbath School teacher no more to this day, nor
ever intend to be one again, after such a fashion.
"The carnal mind is enmity against God, and is not
subject to the law of God, neither indeed can be."

CHAPTER VII.

Not long after this my desire of finding living christians increased. I had now been in search of some for from eighteen to twenty months, but had not been able to find any. I had been hunting them among Baptists of various kinds, Campbellites, Methodists, Universalists; at camp-meetings, basket-meetings, picnic-meetings, prayer-meetings, mission-ary-meetings, and many other kinds of meetings, but all to no purpose. One day, in particular, I had been meditating rather much upon this subject, and I began to think that, perhaps after all, I might be in the wrong myself, when immediaiely an arrow of everlasting love reached my poor trembling heart, and the word of the Lord came to me, saying: "Be ye holy, for I am holy"; or rather, it came in the German translation: "Ye *shall* be holy, for I am holy." And, "without holiness, no man shall see the Lord!" I saw at once, in the twinkling of an eye, *Jesus* to be my holiness. He was to me the same Jesus yesterday and to-day—the same forever. Now I thought if I was to find no people of God in this great country, I verily must dwell alone. Be it so; if Jesus was but precious to me, I possessed heaven on earth, and I want no more. When I had now concluded to go out no more in search of be-lievers, I was determined to learn to read English.

That same day my neighbor, a schoolmaster, met me going home at noon, and the thought struck me, that perhaps he might have time to instruct me at nights in reading English. I proposed it to him, and he replied that he would teach me, and that I should come over to his house that same (Saturday) night.

Accordingly I went and he had his books ready. I told him I did not care for reading any other book than the Bible. He got it for me, and I opened it, and began to read where it had fallen open. (Heb. 1.) "God, who at sundry times and in divers manners, spake in times past unto the fathers by the prophets, hath in these last days spoken unto us by his Son, whom he hath appointed heir of all things, by whom also he made the worlds, who, being the brightness of *his glory* and *the express image of his person*, and upholding all things by the word of his power, when he had by himself purged our sins, sat down on the right hand of the majesty on high." Here I began to talk about what I had been reading to the teacher and his wife, and instead of being an obedient scholar, I turned, (as they afterwards expressed themselves) preacher to the two people. And when I was done, having indeed been able in my own feelings to gaze awhile at the brightness of the glory of the immaculate Lamb of God, yea, the express image of the person of God—the teacher said : " I think you believe the same doctrine my

father and mother believe." I inquired, " Where
do your father and mother live?" He said, "About
half a mile from this place." I shut the book, and
said : " Dear Sir, I thank you for the information ;
I don't think I want to learn any more to-night."
Nor did I ever go as much as once again. The intelligence of there being yet two people that believed
and talked as I did served for all, and my desire to
learn to read any better, had lost its savor. What
I had been seeking, and inquiring for, for years—
behold, I was to find it within half a mile from my
house. And the very day I had given up all hopes
of finding any that had learned of the Father to
speak the 'pure language of Canaan and to pro-
nounce the " Shibboleth " of christian experience
tremblingly and rejoicingly—I was made to hear
that there lived a few almost within reach. The
whole night I spent in praising God for his loving
kindness to his unprofitable worm.

Early on Sunday morning I made ready to visit
the aforesaid believers, who were said to believe the
same doctrine that I did. I need not say here that
I went with a prayerful heart, supplicating the
throne of grace to let me find favor with the two
precious souls, and to make it manifest to me, that
they truly loved the Lord. I stepped in the house,
and the dear old folks looked somewhat surprised
that Bernard the tailor (as they called me there fa-
miliarly) came to them so early in the morning.

They bade me sit down, and I looked full in their
faces. I thought I discovered looks of sincerity in
both of their countenances. I began immediately
to tell them that I was a Baptist, but I differed from
all worldly minded people, Baptist or otherwise, and
ever since I had been inquiring for a few who believed like I did, and that only last night "your son
Andrew told me, that I would find in you such folks
as I desired to find." The old people intimated
that they were Baptists, but that they differed in
their views on doctrine from all the religious
sects in the world, in fact they belonged to the
sect everywhere spoken against. I saw the old
Bible which had the appearance of being used
frequently, took it in my hand and said, " If you
belong to this sect everywhere spoken against, I
believe you belong to the innumerable company,
the church of the living God, which the world
cannot see and which is not of this world." I
opened the book, and it fell open at the Psalms.
I began to read and to talk as I went along. Every
passage, yea, every word was made glorious to me ;
O I discovered Jesus in every line. After I had
been talking some time, I looked at the old people,
and behold the old brother wept. The tears rolled
down his cheeks, and the old lady whom I regarded
as a mother in Israel was melted very much, and
then I wept with them, and I had found that the
dear Lord had made these two people manifest to

my conscience as sincere lovers of the Lord Jesus
Christ. Now I wanted to leave; but they would
not let me go. I must stay for dinner, and I must
go and get my wife, too, and stay all day; and then
they wanted me to preach to them, (as they called
my talk) all the time. When I was once by myself
I could find neither words, nor exultation to praise
my dearest Lord ; words seemed too weak. I could
only say with exceeding great joy, " Praise the Lord,
praise the Lord, O my soul, praise the Lord !" We
stayed all day with them till late at night, and when
we left, they told us we must come next Sunday and
they would take us in their big wagon to meeting.
Next Sunday we went, became acquainted with the
Old School Baptists at the Clover Church, Clover
Association. Elder Brooks was pastor of the Clover
church. I think his text the first morning I heard
him preach was, " Thou shalt be called, sought out,
a city not forsaken.''

From what I could gather I was satisfied that
sound doctrine was here maintained, and after
preaching, myself and wife stayed at Elder Brooks
that day, and became acquainted with a deacon of
the Clover church, brother Wm. Laycock, who was
made very dear to my soul, because he did talk better to my understanding than any one else present.

A little over two years and a half I had been living in this country. From time to time had been
trying to persuade my parents to send our little boy

we had left in their care, and for which they had
funds sent them and friends recommended, who
would take the child and bring him safe across the
ocean. But when they would not send him with
strangers, and none of my brothers desired to come,
I wrote to my parents that I would send the child's
mother and she under God's blessing would bring
him. Then my parents answered, that, hard as it
was for them to part with the little one, they would
now not keep him from us any longer, and by the
time we received that letter, father had seen them
off from the seaport (Bremerhaven.) My youngest
brother, then a lad of twenty, having the child in
charge, and had pledged himself to watch over him
and not to leave him from his side, night or day.
They were coming over in a steamship, and not as
ourselves had traveled in a sailing-vessel. Thus we
had the privilege of living in expectation of soon
seeing again the only babe God had given us, and
we had left it now about three years, which made
the child nearly seven years old when he would be
with us again, in the same country, and village
and home with us, to have and to keep him, as
long as the Lord in mercy might spare our lives.
The news of the child's coming soon spread, and
some of the neighbors cried for joy, and prayed and
hoped that the loved ones might get home safely. I
was astonished at the sympathy manifested by all
who knew us. We had never imagined that we

were worthy of the notice of people. One morning
my employer came in the shop and asked me: "Did
you tell me the name of the ship your child and
brother come in is ———?" I told him yes, that
was the name. " Well," said he, " that ship is reported lost. It sank in sight of Southampton with
all aboard." I looked up at him now, and saw that
he looked pale and distressed. Just at the moment
when I was about to give way to uncontrolable grief,
I heard distinctly in my heart these words: " Believe only, the child is safe!" A sudden reaction in
my feelings took place, as in a moment, and I said,
being very calm now, to Mr. Hitch: " Well, now I
believe the child is destined to come here anyhow."
Mr. H. said no more. The next morning the news in
the papers was confirmed, and when I told my wife
what wonderful revelation I had had upon the subject, and the promise of God, my wife did not believe
the awful news of the child's destruction either; but
with me, trusted in the deliverance which God was
soon to make manifest to us. Time passed on, however; wife's sister from Cincinnati came to see us, as
she supposed, to weep and mourn with us, but she
found us in good cheer, and was utterly astonished at
our strange conduct, as she called it. On the morning
of the 4th of July, however, we were all to be made
happy. I was in the shop between 5 and 6 o'clock
in the morning, when I looked out of doors, and lo!
there right before me in the road, I saw my brother

standing, holding by the hand a little boy, as big again as the babe we had left. With one bound, jumping over six or seven steps at once, I leaped right in front of my child, took him in my arms, and said, " Is your name Justus Greenwood ?" " Yes, sir," said he ; and brother said to him, "This is your papa, who left you at grandpapa's." But no, he could not believe it, I took him in my arms and brought him to his mother, and said : " Here, my dear ; here he is. God is good. Extol his glorious name forever and ever."

PART III.

MY EXPERIENCE IN THE MINISTRY.

CHAPTER I.

My calling and experience in the ministry, being so closely interwoven with all my life, I have chosen to inform the church of it in this the third part of my travels in the wilderness. When my little boy and brother had safely arrived, upon questioning my brother, he gave us an explanation as to how they had escaped from being drowned, as was supposed or reported by the newspapers. He said, when their ship from Germany landed at Southampton, the passengers were told that they might for an hour or two look at the town, and then they were to be transferred to another steamer, their ship having been ordered to take in grain for some other port. And when they were all gone on board the other vessel, they themselves saw their first ship leave port, and it had not gone very far when it began to sink so sudden, and of course they saw it no more. Thus God had in mercy spared *all* the passengers, and all arrived in this country without any trouble or accident.

Now all my desires, prayers and supplications had been answered, the *Lord* in mercy having dealt bountifully with me, and I verily supposed I might go on smoothly from henceforth.

I divided the work I had to do in my trade with my brother, he being of the same occupation with me, and had also learned his trade under me. About this time, when all was calm in my formerly troubled heart, I never shall forget the words that came to me, when busy at my work one day, and engaged in conversation not religious at all. I was standing at my table cutting out some garments, when the following words were fastening within like a nail in a sure place: " And Jesus himself began to be about thirty years of age." Luke 3:23.   At first I intended to think no more about the words. I tried to forget them, but they followed me; they were repeated to me at my work, at meals, yea in my sleep at nights, until at last I perceived and believed that the words were impressed on my mind by the Holy Spirit, and I cried: " What then, Lord ?"   I now read the connection, and saw that about at that time Jesus began his ministry. I myself lacked about two months of being thirty years of age, and was not able what to make or think of the impression. Such

words in the Bible could have nothing to do with
my hitherto unprofitable career in life. Meeting-
time arrived once more, and wife and child went
with me to meeting. My wife at that time was not
a Baptist. The people from far and near had expected us to be there, and I had previously united
with the Clover church, which had received me on
my experience. Several Elders from Ohio and Kentucky met with us, and I had the privilege of conversing with them all. They all unanimously declared they believed that the Lord had separated
me for the ministry. I told them, if so, the dear
Lord might not expect me to try to speak in English; this, God knew, I said, would always be utterly impossible for me to do. I could never learn
enough to declare his great goodness in a tongue
foreign and strange to me. But oh! if it would
please his Majesty, our adorable King, to call me in
the German gospel-field, if there were any such in
this country, I thought I could forsake everything,
and give myself wholly to the work. I knew the
Lord would provide for me and mine in this world,
but, I said, I knew also that in the English tongue
I should never dare to try. No indeed, I would
never be able to find words to express my thoughts,
feelings, ups and downs, and to tell the people what
I knew of Jesus and his love. And all the many
brethren I met with at that meeting showed plainly
to my understanding that they loved me with God's

love! The old people treated us like we were their own children, and those of my own age, like brethren in brotherly love and brotherly kindness. I went home from that meeting with a grateful heart, and cheerfully conversed with wife and child about this people, and said: "They are the same people I joined in Germany." And she, too, was convinced of this, and told me she thought this people showed their true love to one another and to us more than they in Germany. But I said: "Child, this is so because these people here are not interfered with when they worship God according to the dictates of God's word and Spirit, but you see how they are hooted down in the old country, and are almost shy at one another when they meet in the street, for fear of being ill-treated for it; which they can ill afford; being so dreadful poor, they must not be thrown out of employment for any open demonstration of christian love-tokens in the midst of a gainsaying world. But I assure you when they met together in their solemn assembles, alone, as it were, with their own God, their love was manifested by having Christ dwell in their hearts, and in speaking richly to one another of their all-conquering Saviour Christ; and with many tears of gratitude to God have I witnessed the presence of Jesus among them.

The next meeting in August, 1857, the pastor of the church at Clover had gone to the Association

somewhere. I walked some five or six miles to get
to meeting on Saturday. Arriving there, I found
most of the male members sitting out of doors conversing about the things of this world. This seemed
strange to me, and I said: " Brethren, would you
permit me to tell you, that you herein differ a little
from the brethren in Germany. When they meet
together for worship, it is not to talk about this
world and the things of this world, but they converse
with one another about eternal things, belonging to
the eternal world or kingdom of Jesus Christ." All
at once one of the brethren said something about
sitting in conference; and then and there gave Bro.
Greenwood license or liberty to preach in the Old
School Baptist Church anywhere. I trembled from
head to foot. I thought I had done wrong, yet managed, by request, to give out a hymn, and stammer-
ing a few broken sentences in prayer, and tried to
talk a little while of the great love of God, wherewith he had loved his people, though they were his
foes, and dead in trespasses and in sins—and to this
day I verily believe not one understood my broken
sentences. I felt so ashamed of myself that I concluded that I would never attempt to open my
mouth again, as far as the English language was
concerned; yea, I entreated the most gracious Lord
to forgive me, and blot out this presumption of
mine, and I promised the Lord I would never do so
again. I went home and my companion saw there

was something wrong. I told her our stay at Clover,
I thought, was at an end. The church had set me
at liberty to preach, and I was persuaded the church
had made a mistake. I had tried, and would never
try again in English. Oh! the rebellion of my heart.
Sure

> "Blind unbelief is sure to err,
>   And scan God's works in vain,
>   God is his own interpreter,
>   And he will make it plain."

CHAPTER II.

I concluded to quit the business at Clover and go
back to Cincinnati, to find out if the Lord had called
me to the ministry. If so, the Germans would receive me. I would go first alone, and leave my family
at Clover. Having bought the house we lived in and
paid for it, we would have no rent to pay; and I
would try to find ease for my troubled conscience
about preaching. Monday morning I had my machine and other necessary tools packed, and went off
to the German gospel field, as I supposed. To rent
a little room in Cincinnati and to find work, required
but a few hours. I soon also found the German
(Missionary) Baptists, conversed with a good many
of them, and found them very intelligent as to their

6

church organization, Sabbath schools, missions, theological institutions, etc., etc.   But these things had no weight with me.   I cared for none of them, and did not seek after such things.   I spoke to some, nay, *all* I came in contact with, about the one more excellent way, and talked of Christ and his unspeakably great love to perishing sinners.   But this seemed to have no weight with them, and so we differed. Nevertheless, I informed them that I had joined the Old School Baptist church, and that the church had given me the privilege to preach in their churches, but I was sure I could never preach in English, and when I half intimated that I should like to try in my own language, they said they were glad of it, but I would have to go to school first, and when the board was satisfied, they might send me forth as a missionary preacher, or evangelist, or colporteur, tract distributor, or some such thing.   Oh, my poor heart!   I felt it, as it were, sinking fathoms, for all such things were sickening to me.

I was working at my trade, when on the third day one old, dear believing brother, whose name was Krueger, came to see me.   He could talk no English at all.   He said he had heard of me, and wished to speak with me.   He began at once and told me, with tears, how he had been apprehended of Christ Jesus in the old country ; and how he had been brought in guilty before God ; how the dear Lord Jesus had at last forgiven him all his sins, and how God had wiped away all tears from his eyes. Blessed be God, I felt a union to this loving and living man! O, says I, Bro. K., this city is too oppressive for us to converse about the things pertaining to our salvation. Let us go outside of the city and take a long walk on the road, and then we will tell one another much of Jesus and his power to save, and talk of the goodness of our God!

So said, so done; and when we were outside of the city, we had a great feast all by ourselves, and our hearts too did burn within us, for we believed Jesus conversed with us, and we both wept together and rejoiced together. He told me also how he had, for the want of anything better, joined himself to the Missionary (German) church of that city, but he could not live on the husks, they all sought so eagerly to devour. This brother came to see me every day after working hours (he being a cooper by trade) as long as I remained in the place.

One day the preacher called me off, and wanted me to stay with him. I went. I tried to converse with him, but could not. He would not allow me to have any opinion of mine; he acted as though he thought I knew nothing at all about anything. He endeavored hard to impart some instruction to me, as to what I had to do in order to become quite popular with his people. And the first thing he said which I must do, was to quit forever those straight-jackets (as he called the Old School Bap-

tists) and formally join his society. Next thing he
said was, that I must convert my wife. He was astonished at me, for me to talk about preaching, when
I had as yet never converted my wife. What! A
preacher with an unconverted wife! Awful, awful
indeed! I told him I had never tried to convert
her. I did not think she needed conversion. She
was all to me that the Lord had intended she should
be, a good wife—as her own father often had told
me, one of the best of his eleven children. And if
God would have her in the church of Christ, he
would at his own time call her and bring her to
Zion. This the preacher called monstrous doctrine.
Well, I saw I was in the wrong pew again. My
preacher friend, who proved himself to be an enemy
according to the gospel, nevertheless treated me very
kindly. This was on Saturday evening. After this
brief conversation, he said I must excuse him for to-
night, he had to go to his study and look over his
sermon a little while. I was left alone the remainder
of the night, and also Sunday morning until the
first bell began to ring for their Sabbath School, and
I must accompany them to see their nice school. I
did so. Finding nothing at all of importance, I
looked on till preaching time. Then I became an
attentive listener. At the end of his discourse, the
preacher told his congregation what an awful sin it
was for one professing christianity to clean his boots
on Sunday morning, looking straight at me all the

while, for I had been that very morning found guilty
of that awful deed in his own yard. I saw horror
depicted on the cou'ntenance of some, but on my old
brother Krueger's face beamed hopefulness, that I
might be able to answer the preacher when he .was
through. As soon as he stopped, I got up and told
the folks not to look so ho. rified. I asked them, and
quoted Matthew 12: 3—8. Jesus himself was with
his disciples when they were an hungered, and began to pluck the ears of corn and to eat, and that
on the Sabbath day. While I was speaking, the
preacher made motions with his hands several times
to stop me, but he did not stop me; and when I
told them all in conclusion, that it were better for
all that hear me to-day to have faith in Christ, than
to be led about by blind leaders of the blind, they
would hear no more, but old brother Krueger
jumped up and said: "Brother Greenwood is on the
Lord's side, and I go with him." Then order was
restored, and the congregation was dismissed by the
pastor. The next morning (Monday) Bro. K. went
with me to Clover. I took him then to church, and
told him he soon would learn English enough to
understand this people. And when we came to the
church, I told the church all my intention to desert
them, and the reason why, and what had come of it.
And then I spoke of the goodness of God, and that
the dear Lord, instead of frowning me down, had
compassion on me, for he had given me this sheep of

his fold to bring to his mother's house, to make
merry in the precious faith of the Son of God. There
was joy in that church that day. And Bro. K. was
satisfied in his own mind, and desired to unite with
the church, if the church would hear his experience,
myself acting as interpreter. The church was willing, and then Bro. Krueger called on me for us both
to kneel down in the open space of the meeting-
house, and for me to lead in prayer in our own (German) language. Prayer being ended, many weeping in the house, we arose to our feet and stood before the congregation, and with trembling Bro. K.
told his great experience of his sinnership, and the
grace of God which had been so abundant with him,
I, in the meantime, interpreting sentence for sentence until he was through. I never saw more tears
shed than at that melting meeting that afternoon,
for it was long in the afternoon when the meeting
finally closed, and Bro. Krueger was received with
gladness of heart by all the church.

CHAPTER III.

The Clover Association was to be held with the
Brush Creek Church that year, and brethren from
our (Clover) church invited me to go with them to
the Association. This was the first meeting of that

kind I had the privilege to attend, and I went with
the brethren. Here I heard a great deal of preaching and conversation, which helped me much every
way. Here also I came to the conclusion that I
should want to live in a community where there
was a little church, and I might have the opportunity to meet with a few if possible every Sunday,
and I found a few brethren who cordially invited
me to come to Lynchburg, Ohio, where there was a
meeting-house, and the church would meet there at
least twice in the month. They wanted their
preacher to visit other destitute churches also, and
I went to see the place, became acquainted with
some of the members, and made up my mind to
move to Lynchburg.

About this time an indifference fell upon me that
I could not account for. I called it a horror of
great darkness. I could not pray, talk or converse
with any one. Spiritual life seemed to have left
me. For a long time I remained in this darkness.
I had no communion with the blessed Saviour. No
word could I obtain from the Captain of my salvation. He was at a distance now, and I went along
groping for the wall, as it is written, " We grope for
the wall like the blind, and we grope as though we
had no eyes; we stumble at noonday as in the
night." Isaiah 59: 10. . I tried to preach. We met
every two weeks. The other time when meeting-
time for other churches arrived, I would travel some

thirty or forty miles on horseback to get there in time; but the peace of God, O where was it? It was far from me. I seemed to live as though I had never known a blessed Saviour in his love to me. I rested in the doctrine of election and predestination in the letter, and was unconcerned as to the spiritual understanding of these precious parts of God's doctrine. Worldly cares and a constant trying to succeed in business took such a hold upon me that I did not see God's hand in anything. I observed nothing pertaining to God and godliness, consequently could not see the loving kindness of the Lord. My brother in the flesh had left us for St. Louis; afterwards he enlisted in the army and was killed at the battle of Fort Donnelson.

Bro. Krueger stayed at Clover a short time after we had left and went to the State of Illinois. Just about the same time we went to Lynchburg, another tailor from Cincinnati also had moved to the same place. But that man died shortly after he came there, and wherever the news went the brethren from afar supposed it to be me, and when I went to Clover once more the brethren said they all had mourned me as dead. O beloved! I seemed to be in my feelings as one twice dead, plucked up by the roots. All the conversation I could participate in now was the letter of the word, or rather portions of it, which as preached by the Old School Baptists agreed with my understanding. I had become, while at Clover, a subscriber for the *Signs of the Times*, but not yet being conversant with the language, there were many things in it hard to be understood by me. Alas! alas! my poor heart remained "unfeeling and unmoved." Could I but quit trying to preach, (O how often was this thought suggested to my mind), all might be easy, and I might get on as well as any one else in this world. But that appeared to be impossible. I would go the very days that were to be considered the very best days for my business. What made me go? I could not tell at that time. Once I went to Clover (some thirty odd miles) on horse-back, and as I was riding along some passage of Scripture about the love of God was given and entered directly as it were in my life. It melted me to tears once more; tears of godly sorrow and joy alternately. I began to think that may be after all the Lord had called me to the ministry. I thought I surely would be able to talk of this love-visit of the Lord Jesus to *me*, his most unprofitable servant. Arriving at the meeting-house, the smile of love, joy and peace was still manifest in my weeping eyes. The pastor and brethren seemed to be quite overjoyed at seeing me come once more so unexpectedly among them. Being called up into the stand, I began to tell of the goodness of God, when suddenly all the sweetness and savor of Jesus' name was taken or withheld from me. I stopped and told the congregation it was of

no use, I could tell them nothing now. The dear
Lord had in former times been very gracious to me,
but of late he had withdrawn his loving countenance from me, and then all I can do is to fall dead
at his feet.   But though at present I could tell them
nothing, I knew one thing, that I loved him and
his people and his truth, and that it was the love of
God that had brought us together that day, and I
felt in my heart that I loved this beloved congregation for Jesus' sake.   Out of my great darkness a
light shone.   I saw old and young weep, and then
I wept, too, and with tears I told them of the love-
visit of Jesus Christ to my soul that very day, and
how I had thought I'd been able to tell them about
it; but alas! I had made such a failure of it.   After
the close of that meeting, the brethren and sisters
agreed that this had been one of the best meetings
they had had for a long time, and they prayed God
(they said) that he would make me an able minister of the New Testament.

At another time I went to Cæsar's Creek church
and became acquainted with many brethren there,
and an old brother in Jesus who could not hear
preaching, but would go to meeting and judge of
the preaching by the countenances of preachers and
brethren, as to how the news from Paradise was received by them.   The old brother looked at me,
while I made the attempt to address the congregation : gradually his countenance became pleased—it

fairly beamed with joy. After preaching he took
me by the hand and said that I must go home with
him: he felt that the Lord had me in hand, and
said he, " I have many things to say to you." Bro.
Hatch (for that was his name) could hear a very
little, especially when his wife spoke to him. He
said he understood me altogether. Mine was heart
religion. I spoke from the heart, and he could notice that in my countenance. He told me much of
heavenly things, and the time slipped away so soon.
I had determined to be at home on Sunday night,
and here I was 33 miles from home on Sunday afternoon at 3 o'clock. Then they had to admonish
me to be off, if I would not stay till morning. And
very reluctantly I parted from this beloved child of
God and his family, the old brother himself came
out with me and assisted me to get on the pony ;
then he said, " Here, my brother, here is a little for
you to bear your expenses; and now be of good
cheer, the Lord has chosen you to bear his name
before the people, and my prayers are with you.
May Abraham's God be your shield, and your exceeding great reward. Remember Abraham's God
is our God, and he will be our guide even unto
death !" Then I went off, filled to overflowing with
the remembrance of such .kindness and brotherly
love bestowed upon me, the poorest of the flock of
God.

Having stayed a few years in that region of coun-

try, I found that my stay there was at an end. I
went to Cincinnati again in search of a situation as
cutter. When I stepped off of the cars at the depot,
there was a man there who knew me, and after the
usual inquiring about me and mine, I told him
what I had come for, and he said he was just in
search of such an one as myself, for he had been requested to send a man of my qualifications to
Charleston, W. Va., and if I would go there all
would be right. I told him I would go, wrote home,
and the next day I arrived in Charleston. This
was in 1860. After promising to go to work the
next morning, I went in search of a boarding-house,
and soon found one. When at dinner the landlord
let fall a word or two by which I noticed he must
be a baptized believer. I asked him did he belong
to the Old School Baptist Church, and he said yes
he did, and I stretched out my hand to him over
the table, and told him that that blessed church
held also such an one as myself. He asked me was
I a preacher? I told him " No, no, not that;" and
then informed him how, about three years ago, the
church had set me at liberty to exercise my gift, if
there be any gift. When Sunday came, we both
went out to the meeting-house in the country, a place
some five or six miles out of town. We were a little late, and the preacher, Bro. Martin, had just begun to preach. I heard him through, and heard
him with delight. My tears flowed freely, and my

poor heart once more rejoiced in God my Saviour. When he stopped, he came down from the pulpit to me, and he said he believed I was a preacher, and an Old School Baptist: I must come in the stand and say something. I could not refuse, and went with him in the stand. Through a mist of tears I brought forth a few utterances, after which the whole congregation welcomed and greeted me as though they had known me always. I became warmly attached to this people, and visited them every meeting day Saturdays and Sundays, rain or shine. The war broke out, and for a time I had to obtain a pass to go through the picket line, stationed some four miles from Charleston; but never found any trouble to meet with the dear people.

Almost every able bodied man enlisted in either one or the other army; the warriors asked me, too, why I did not enlist and shoulder the musket? I gave them the principal reason, viz: that I belonged to a kingdom that was not of this world, and I found it impossible to serve two masters, flesh and Spirit, at the same time.

About this time I had great rejoicing in my heart, because I had learned that a few German believers at Albany, N. Y., had received the grace of God, and had become obedient to the gospel of God's eternal love, and had united with the church of God. I wrote them a few words of encouragement in the German tongue, and some one of the brethren had

my letter to them translated in the English and
published in the *Signs of the Times.* At this time I
had made the acquaintance of a few humble brethren who lived in the town of Charleston. They were
colored brethren, but they were taught of God. We
had conversed together at various times, though
they would not come in my house ; but they found
a nice hall for us to meet in, and I tried to tell them
out of the Scriptures, by way of what they called
preaching, concerning the kingdom and the King,
the Saviour and his great salvation. They desired
me to break bread to them, but not being ordained,
I could not comply. I brought the case to the Lynchburg church, where my membership then was, and
they wrote me to come over. I went. They called
a presbytery, consisting of Elders Brooks and Hite,
and the brethren all being satisfied, ordained me to
the work of the ministry on the 23rd of March, 1861.

CHAPTER IV.

In 1862 I left Charleston for Hillsboro, Ohio. Here
I settled down an entire stranger, without means
and without friends. I selected that town because it
was ten and thirteen miles from two places of meeting, to which I might walk if I was not able to hire
a horse. I opened my business in that place, and

rented a room adjoining a shoemaker's shop. This gentleman told me that he himself was a Missionary Baptist, and he desired sometimes conversation on religious subjects with me. In consequence of which he called me a Regular Hard Shell Baptist. One of his preachers came in to see him one day, and nothing would do but I must be introduced to his preacher. He introduced me as one of the hardest Hard Shells he had ever met with. The preacher laughed, and said it was all right, that he was an Old School Baptist also. I told him I had most assuredly understood him to be introduced to me as a Missionary Baptist. "Well," says he, "I preach here for this people," and then began to talk about means and the use of means, etc., and he then said he thought that there was no difference as far as the doctrine was concerned. I answered, "The difference between truth and error is as great as light and darkness, heaven and hell." We did not agree, and he stuck to the means. He now disputed almost every passage that I was enabled to bring to his notice. At last he lost his patience, and left apparently in ill humor. He came back almost instantly. Having discovered my name on a little sign-board out of doors, he came in the room, walked the floor up and down, and called my name two or three times. Then he said: "That name ought to be drywood or dead-wood." I sighed, and said within myself, "Lord, have I Scripture to overthrow this delusion?" The

Scripture was applied at once, and I stepped up to him, and said: "Why, dear sir, ought my poor name be that?" He said, "Because the doctrine you preach is dry and dead." I answered, how can that be, when the Author of that glorious doctrine calls himself the "Green Tree?" for he says, if they do these things on the green tree, what will they do on the dry? He reached out his hand, and said: "You beat me again; may we meet in heaven."

At Hillsboro I was remarkably blessed in Providence. I soon obtained a reasonable share of the business, bought a house and lot, horse and buggy, all paid for, and consequently came to the conclusion that I was always to live there, and die in my nest. Job 29 : 18. But I soon found I had as yet no certain dwelling place.

In 1865 I sold out and moved again to Cincinnati. Here I got acquainted with Brethren Howell and Danks. With them I have spent many a blessed hour, and have been at their house at times with my family. We would go together to meetings as often as we could. Brother Danks has since become a minister of the gospel in the Old School Baptist Church. Their labors of love which they have bestowed upon me and mine, will never be forgotten by me. While at Cincinnati my wife had been on a visit to Brush Creek church, where my membership then was. She had given in her experience there and was received by the church and baptized (immersed) by the pastor, Elder Daniel Bradley, from Kentucky.

In the fall of 1865 I moved from Cincinnati to Madison, Indiana. I found no Baptists in the place. We did not like to live there. I wrote to Deacon Hargrove, whose name I had seen in the *Signs of the Times*, desiring him to tell me where I might find Baptists in Indiana. He answered me in a touching letter, that he knew of none nearer than about one hundred miles from Madison. There, he knew, lived an old preacher whose name was Elder Benjamin Keith. He sent me also a map showing where the old brother lived. I wrote to Elder Keith, telling him what great desire I had to see him. His answer was encouraging.

I gave up my situation of one hundred dollars per month, and told my employers that I had no rest night nor day till I could live again in a community of Baptists and be with believing brethren. They marveled at this. They wanted me to stay, but I told them, no, I cannot stay. Jer. 20: 8. I boarded the boat for Louisville, and then walked some eighteen miles, and found my dear old father Keith. I spent several days in his company. He took me in his buggy to meetings, and I realized once more that my spirit rejoiced in God my Saviour.

When I departed from old Brother Keith, I went to see old Brother Hargrove also. On my way I became acquainted with some Means and Duty-Faith Baptists, who could not understand my speech. On reaching Brother Hargrove's I found him to be one likeminded with myself.

I had now traveled several hundred miles, and my funds being spent I did not know how I should reach home again without writing home to my wife to send me some money. Deacon Hargrove, however, advised me to take the cars to Evansville, where I would find a little church. He bought me a ticket and gave me five dollars besides; and when I was on the cars I felt that God in his providence had once more provided for me. Oh, would he now also provide for me in his grace and fill my heart with heavenly knowledge and wisdom, and let me find favor with his dear people at the place where I was to find true Baptists, without an *if* or *but*, or *yea* and *nay*, or any of manual things. For the gospel of our God is not *manual* or *man with us*, but *Immanuel, God with us.* And the Lord hearkened and heard, and he gave me then and there brokenness of heart and contrition of spirit, and I could once more sit at Jesus's feet, clothed and in my right mind, and thus I was strengthened in the inner man.

I sought and found the dear people, who immediately made it known among themselves and appointed a meeting for me, and I tried to preach to them in their meeting house six times in succession

amidst great rejoicing to us all. Some of them exclaimed aloud after meeting, that they praised God
that the voice of the turtle was once more heard in
the land. When they found out it was my desire
to come to Evansville to live, they pressed me for
an answer upon their urgent invitation to come to
their city. I could not at once obtain a plain answer from the "Oracle," (Psalm 28: 2,) so as to be
satisfied myself whether it be the Lord's will or not
for me to come among them. Late Sunday night,
when nearly all the members had gathered together
in one place, they were anxious for an answer, and
I told them at last that if I could find a house suit-
able for me and mine to live in before eight o'clock
in the morning, then I would rent it and come to
their city. This now was understood by all, and
towards midnight we separated, after praying with
and for one another, and singing and conversing till
then. Early in the morning, Bro. Clark and myself
went in search of a house. We strolled towards the
meeting-house; near there lived also several of the
brethren. About a square and a half from the meeting-house, we saw some people moving out of a nice
little brick house, and I said to Bro. Clark, that
house would do very well ; that will suit me exactly.
We inquired for the owner, and found that he lived
a few miles in the country, and that he was one of
my own countrymen. They also told us to tell the
owner that not since late last night had they had

any notion to leave the house, and that only this morning early had concluded to vacate.

We walked out in the country and found the owner at home, and we told him what his renters had said; and he said, " Well, you can have the house." The price of the rent was agreed on, and all was satisfactory. Then I went on the boat, several of the brethren saw me off, and we parted very affectionately. The next day I arrived home, and wife and son (who was by this time learning his trade) were glad to see me after more than four weeks' stay from home. I told them all now, and declared that Evansville was a tolerably large city, and there was also a little church there, and I had concluded to move to that place at once. Wife said folks wanted me to stay at an increased salary. But when I told her I could work on salary no longer, because of my heavenly calling, which I must not be disobedient to, she rather feared we might not do so well as we had done hitherto. But when she saw there was no help for it, she consented cheerfully, trusting all would come right in the end.

Arriving at Evansville, we soon had our household stuff hauled to the house, and the next day I went in search of a place for my boy at his trade, and found a good place for him at once. Then I went into a clothing store and found work as cutter for myself. The Lord was graciously pleased to bless our little meetings, and every now and then some were added to the church. Elder Macer was pastor, and he came once a month.

Three or four months had thus passed away in blessedness and peace; joy and love were marked fruits of the Spirit among us all. As I was returning one day from an appointment in the country, in going to the post office I received a letter. I opened it, and saw it was closely written. I stepped into the new merchant tailor establishment from New York, (who had also a New York cutter at a salary of two thousand dollars a year, and whom I had not yet seen, but desired to make so great a man's acquaintance.) I found the Missionary Baptist preacher earnestly conversing with the cutter, and when I came in the room the preacher left. Then I told the old gentleman I was a tailor, and just now I desired to sit down a little while and read a religious letter I had received from a lady unknown to me. He placed a chair for me to sit down. I became interested while reading the letter (it was a spiritual epistle from Sister Kate Bartley, Laconia, Ind.) The cutter asked me what kind of religion I professed. I told him I was an Old School Baptist. His eyes brightened up, saying, "I have heard of them: they have a little church in this city, I have understood, and I have thought I would go and hear them some Sunday." I said, "I suppose you are a Missionary Baptist?" "Oh, no," he answered, "I am a member of the Strict Baptist church, England." I told him I had heard of the Strict Baptists in England, and had believed that they were the same people that were called Primitive Baptists in the South, and in the North they went by the name of Old School Baptists. We talked a little, and I called his attention to the difference there was between the doctrine of grace and the grace of the doctrine: the former may be held in the mere intelligence with cordial assent and consent to the truth, "and their mouths speak great swelling words, having men's persons in admiration because of advantage." But the true believer possesses the grace of the doctrine, (yea, verily, the election hath obtained it,) and this precious grace brings salvation to the soul; it brings Jesus into his heart, and the Father's love in Jesus. Grace brings consolation to his dejected spirit and light into his dark mind. Yea, it brings salvation to the uttermost! A Triune Jehovah, Father, Son and Holy Ghost, and all that he is in covenant to him as a poor lost sinner. Oh precious grace! He brings in the heart its saving power in such a way that the poor lost sinner feels himself a saved sinner through the election, redemption and regeneration of a Three One-God! "The letter killeth, but the spirit giveth life."

While I was talking to the old gentleman, I looked at him, and lo! the tears rolled over his cheeks, and I felt that he had the grace of God in his heart.

Then I bid him God speed, and made as to depart,
but he held me by the hands, asked me if I wanted
work. I said, " No, not just now," I worked somewhere else. He wished to know who preached at
our meeting-house on Sundays, and I told him come
and see. Some little preacher tries to say something,
but our object in meeting together is for spiritual
worship, and our congregation were all good singers
too. The following Sunday the old brother came
in. I was giving out the first hymn. He stood still
in the door and looked at me awhile, rubbed his
glasses to convince himself, and then, as he afterwards
told me, sat down with a fluttering, trembling heart.
He said he had never as much as thought even that
myself might be that little preacher whom I had
almost called insignificant. Yet he was now ever
so glad that he came and heard me. And his wife
too spoke likewise. Now a friendship sprang up
between us that was more than earthly friendship.
We felt and confessed to one another that we were
brethren in one precious Saviour, Jesus Christ, our
dearest Lord. Oh, how good was the Lord to us!
In his shop we were often together enjoying ourselves in heavenly conversation. His love to the
truth was deep and lasting as the everlasting hills,
because it was in Christ, towards Christ, and by
Christ. Oh, how glad was I that the dear Lord had
led me to Evansville.

CHAPTER V.

Many times in going home and coming from this man of God have I shed tears of gratitude to God for having made me acquainted with this dear child of his. His name was John Mott. His family I had not as yet visited. One day Bro. M. met me on the street, and his face beamed with joy. He did not see me at first, but I hailed him, looked him in the face, shook a cordial handshake, and questioned him only with my eyes as to say, " What cheer?" He understood me; he held my hand firm, and I saw tears falling from his eyes—tears of joy, and I still wondering what it all could mean. Then he says, " Rejoice with me, dear sir, my daughter is under conviction." " Come," said I, " tell me all about it." We went to his place of work, and there he began to tell me how, for some time, she had been talking to her mother of her sinfulness, and then for days she had gone about mourning without the sun, her sins meanwhile pressing her so that she was unable to work. At last she had taken her sewing machine in her own room and wanted to be entirely by herself with her great sorrow, for she felt as if she were doomed to destruction. He then told me what a good, pious, industrious child she had always been, and oh! how glad was this father that the Lord had not put her among the Pharisees, but rather shown her that she needed a righteousness above that of the Pharisees, and the Lord had made her one of his sinners whom he saves with an everlasting salvation.

"Now, we know," he continued, "that this is of God, and he that hath begun the good work will also perform it until the day of Jesus Christ." I rejoiced with my beloved brother, and we mingled our tears in thanksgiving and praise to him who doeth all things well. Blessed be his holy name forever and ever. "We concluded to say nothing to her," continued Bro. M., "the Lord having begun, the Lord will continue and the Lord will finish the work to the praise of his grace." "This people have I formed for myself, they shall show forth my praise."

In the meantime the Lord worked among us with signs and wonders. He called several persons out of darkness into his marvellous light, and brought them with weeping and supplication to Zion. I baptized some, while others united with the little body by letter and experience, and both. We were also blessed in our evenings together on Sunday afternoons at one or the other of the brethren's houses. One time Bro. M. and his family, including the daughter under conviction, all went home with us for dinner and all stayed till late in the afternoon.

The sorrowful child did for the most time weep in silence, and listened to our conversation, and when they all went home, I felt that my soul was knitted

7

to that family like David's soul had been to Jonathan's. I was also highly favored with the fellowship of all the church, and to my knowledge there was not one barren among them in the things pertaining to godliness. My wife and myself gave in our letters to this beloved body, and they all held us in very high esteem. I can never forget their love and kindness shown to me and mine, during my entire stay among them. Brother and sister Feldstead from the country, and sister Ann Feldstead from the city, and sister Green, old Mother Caldwell, brother and sister Clark, sister Sanders, and brother Young and sister Young, sisters Nightingale and Jones, brother Jonas Crofts and his wife, sister Elizabeth Crofts, several of whom I had baptized and most of whom I believe are yet living at this present time of writing. Many blessed seasons of joy have we had among so many loved ones. While my heart was full of praise to God, while my soul went forth in songs of thanksgiving and adoration, the church prospering and glorifying God, all going on so full of joy and peace to overflowing—a thunderbolt struck with tremendous force the structure of my heaven on earth.

One morning my son (then nearly 16 years old) and myself went to our work, and on our way I saw how pale he looked. He said : "Papa (he called me always by that name) I feel sick. Have pain in my left leg." I returned home with him and discovered the ankle to be swollen and looked blue and black. Friends and neighbors told us to rub with saltpeter, etc., which I did for about half a day. But he grew worse very rapidly. We called a physician and he said he would soon have him all right again.. But alas! he grew still worse. Sunday while at meeting, my wife being alone watching at his sick-bed, she thought he was dying and came running to the meeting-house just when the congregation was dismissed. I made haste to call two more physicians, the two best ones considered in town, and when they saw the child, declared upon my anxious inquiry that he could not live. O, brethren, my heart, as it were, turned to stone, and if it had not been the Lord on my side then, I should have sank down under this heavy stroke. The child died in four days, all told. I felt myself unable now to do anything. My heart was full of rebellion and I refused to be comforted. In silent despair I concluded : "All is vanity, the Lord hath forsaken me." He has taken my only child away, and I had doted upon him so much and often thought the child's father was no preacher at all, and was not worthy to be one, and that the dear Lord might make a preacher of the boy, he was a so much better child than I had ever been, and that he would do much better than ever his parent could do. But alas! all my hopes were now dashed to the ground as in an instant! O Lord forgive! show pity, show pity, was all I could pray for

days and nights. And what shall I say of his mother?
Oh, thou searcher of all hearts, I believe to this day
that she had more strength and resignation than I
had. I was as one dead; shattered and broken to
shivers. Like a mere machine they took me up and
led me to the omnibus that followed the hearse; I
saw no one, could speak to no one. I thought the
Lord had cast me away as a miserable outcast. I
was no more beloved in His eyes. Then I sank unconscious in the omnibus and had a vision. I thought
some one was leading me by the hand bringing me
to a place I saw at once was a jail. I saw there several such boys as mine, and the question was asked
me: "Was your child better than these?" I answered not a word, I understood not the meaning of
this. Then he led me to a penitentiary and showed
me again several boys of the age of mine, and again
the question was asked, "Do you think your child
was better by nature than these you see now before
you?" I cried, "No, Lord, I believe not." Then he
led me to the gallows, where there were several
youthful murderers ready to be executed. The question again was asked, "Was your child better than
any of these?" "No, Lord," I cried. "By nature we
are all children of wrath, even as others." "Then,"
said my leader, "would you not rather have him
rest in Jesus, and lay him by in peace as you are
now doing, than to see him come to such an end?"
"Yea, Lord," I stammered, "I am reconciled, the

will of the Lord be done." Then I awoke. I dried my tears and promptly we arrived at the place Bro. Felstead had kindly offered us for a resting place. The folks wondered when they saw the change that had taken place with me; and I helped them sing the beautiful hymn Brother Jonas Crofts, a licentiate, in our church, gave out at the grave:

> Asleep in Jesus! Blessed sleep,
> From which none ever wake to weep,
> A calm and undisturbed repose,
> Unbroken by the last of foes.

> Asleep in Jesus! O, how sweet,
> To be for such a slumber meet!
> With holy confidence to sing,
> That death has lost his cruel sting.

> Asleep in Jesus! Peaceful rest,
> Whose waking is supremely blest,
> No fear, no woe, shall dim that hour
> That manifests the Saviour's power.

> Asleep in Jesus! Oh for me
> May such a blissful refuge be;
> Securely shall my ashes lie,
> Waiting the summons from on high.

> Asleep in Jesus! Far from thee,
> Thy kindred and their graves may be;
> But there is still a blessed sleep
> From which none ever wake to weep.

Thus on the 28th of June, 1866, departed our only child, in the 16th year of his age, who had been such a promising child to me. On returning to the house I said, "if I am bereaved I am bereaved;" and then a time of lamentation, mourning and woe followed for days, weeks and months. Oh how unprofitable in the ministry must I have become at that time.

A piece of poetry, the first four verses of which were engraved on his tombstone, was sent to me by a Miss Mattie Watson from Ohio, a daughter of Brother and Sister Watson, with whom we had spent in days past many a profitable hour. I give it here:

> Gone, our morning light,
>   Gone, our evening star;
> Gone, beyond our sight
>   To the land afar.
> Gone, our garden flower,
>   Gone, our daily joy,
> Gone, as in an hour,
>   Gone, our darling boy.
>
> Far, oh, far above,
>   Lands of clouds and storm,
> By the gates of love
>   Rests a shining form,
> Robed in finest white,
>   With the angel throng,
> Crowned with living light,
>   Blest with endless song.
>
> Though like a summer rain
>   Fall the tender leaves,
> Though this heavy pain
>   Gives us no relief,

Though so great our loss,
  Burdening all our care,
Though our daily cross
  Long be hard to bear;

Could we wish him back
  To this world of ours,
Even were life's track
  Through a land of flowers,
Could we wish him here
  Subject long to sin,
Since the heaven so near,
  He has entered in?

Great, oh! great his gain,
  On the blessed shore,
Free from every pain,
  Happy evermore.
Rest then, child of ours,
  With the cherub throng,
Charm the Eden bowers
  With thy sweetest song.

When I received the above precious lines I wrote underneath them, "The Lord hath given, the Lord hath taken away, blessed be the name of the Lord. Though he slay me, yet will I trust in him."

CHAPTER VI.

But the Lord's hand was heavy upon us still. Ps. 32:4. Only two or three days after my child was solemnly put into his grave, Brother and Sister Felstead were at my house, conversing freely about the riches of God's grace in the midst of bereavement, darkness and sorrow, when intelligence was brought the kind parents that one of their children, a boy of 12 or 14 years of age, had come to his death by drowning while bathing in the Ohio river. Oh what a season of sorrow. Oh what a sword pierced through our poor souls. These loved ones had wept with me; now I could weep with them. O blessed, blessed be Jehovah our God, he hath said, "They that sow in tears shall reap in joy." Ps. 126:5.

With a sorrowful heart I tried to speak at the little boy's grave (whom they had laid close to my child) from the words of the Psalmist: "Lord, make me to know mine end, and the measure of my days what it is, that I may learn how frail I am. Behold thou has made my days as an handbreadth, and mine age is as nothing before thee; verily, every man at his best estate is altogether vanity." Psalm 39: 45. Sunday after this, while I was giving out the first hymn, my wife, sister Felstead and sister Burkhart came in the meeting house all dressed in mourning apparel. I had to stop awhile to still the tears that would come. O, beloved reader, I could not see plainly at all times—I could not then discern that our children were embraced in the everlasting arms. Dearest Lord, forgive thy worm all his rebellions and blot out all his iniquities. Oh for the blood of Christ to be applied by the Holy Spirit. This meeting was a meeting more of sighing and crying, than of praise, adoration and hosannahs to the conquering king! The dearest Lord loved his children better than ever their parents could have done. I was so blind and cared not to see. So I could not pray, and knew not what to pray for as I ought, and sometimes I thought that I should yet fall by the hand of my enemy, sin, and sink into irretrievable woe at last. Thus the Lord was teaching me then what gross darkness is, and what it is to be under it, to find out by sad experience " that in me, that is in my flesh dwelleth no good thing."

"Yea, more, with his own hand he seemed
   Intent to aggravate my woe,
Crossed all the fair designs I schemed
   Blasted my gourds and laid me low.

Lord, why is this? I, trembling, cried,
   Wilt thou pursue thy worm to death ?
'Tis in this way, the Lord replied,
   I answer prayer for grace and faith.

These inward trials I employ,
   From self and pride to set thee free;
And break thy schemes of earthly joy,
   That thou may'st find thy all in me."

While in this tribulation, tossed to and fro till the dawning of the day, I met Bro. Mott one morning while going to our work. His countenance bore a pleasing expression. He told me at once that his daughter's mourning days were at end, for the Lord had been pleased to make himself manifest to her. When she had about been given up all hope of ever finding comfort in her sorrow for sin, these words had come to her with saving power: "Cast thy burden upon the Lord, and he shall sustain thee." Psalm 55: 22. At once her mourning turned to joy; she had come down stairs a changed person. The word of Jesus was precious to her now. I replied: Then she will be baptized. Now my advice to you is this: That both you and your wife set a good example before the child, and come over next Saturday and unite with the church; then your daughter will see that you have confidence in the brethren, and I doubt not but that she will then come forward to tell the church what the Lord hath done for her, and be baptized according to the command of our Lord.

On Saturday they all came to the church. First in order came the old brother in Jesus, and stated that he and sister Mott, his wife, both held letters from the strict Baptist church (if I mistake not the name) of London, England, but at the same time they were willing to tell their experience also. And they did and were received. One or two more came

forward, I think, that day, and last of all, I rose up
from my seat, went to where the young sister was,
and told her to come also. I led her by the hand
to her father and mother and before the church.
And she told her experience in plain and simple
language that could be understood by all. And
when she related how the words "Cast thy burden
upon the Lord" had come to her, it seemed to melt
the hardest heart. I baptized her, and one or two
more (I forget now) on Sunday morning in the Ohio
river. Not long after this, our brother Mott fell
sick. He was not able to leave the house for several
months. I visited him towards the last almost
daily. I found him always full of power. I loved
to hear him speak so earnestly and testify with so
much assurance of the grace of God bestowed on
such a poor sinner as he felt himself to be. I admired his conversation; when on his sick bed he
spoke of the achievement of Christ when he subdued the sins of the whole church, which he called
sometimes the whole world; of the dignity and
majesty of the King in the forgiveness of our sins;
of the love of Christ when he laid down his life for
us; of the love of God shed abroad in our hearts
by the Holy Ghost, and all for Jesus' sake; of the
faith of God's elect which God gave us by that grace—

> That pardons crimson sins
> And melts the hardest hearts,
> And from the work it once begins
> It never more departs.

And every time that I was with him, I had the
privilege of kneeling down with the whole family,
and in prayer, praise and supplication made known
our longing desires to our God.   Yea, a very Bethel
was their house to me.   The children, though almost all grown, all loved their parents for the truth's
sake.   And all seemed delighted when they did take
part in the singing and the devotions we were privi-
leged to enjoy.   None of us looked for the end to be
so near, however.   One day I went as usual to see
him, but he had just departed this life in exchange
for life eternal.   He had fallen asleep like an infant,
and his spirit had been at once snatched away in the
embrace of Him whom he had loved here below, because Jesus had loved him first.   Through the kindness of Brother Feldstead a resting place was assigned
the remains by the side of our children.   I endeavored to speak on the occasion from Rev. 14: 13 :
" Blessed are the dead which die in the Lord from
henceforth : yea, saith the Spirit, that they may rest
from their labors; and their works do follow them."

> " Forbear, my friends, to weep:
>   Since death has lost his sting,
>   Those christians that in Jesus sleep,
>   Our God will with him bring."

After meeting one Sunday evening, I felt a great
impression to go to the Missionary (German) Baptist
church.   My wife concluded to go with me; they had
a new preacher, not college-bred, and he preached

a little cheaper for the congregation than the more learned could afford; he had a trade and worked at that some, so we heard others say, and that night we went to hear him for ourselves. When he was through preaching, he called on me to pray. I replied: "I beg to be excused." No, he would not excuse me. I told him and his congregation we were not in the habit of joining with people that went not with us; but he still insisted I might pray with and for them. Then I said: "Let us pray"; and we all knelt down, and I prayed with and for them in my own native language. After this the congregation was dismissed, and I thought no more of the transaction. Some six weeks subsequently a man hailed me on the street. I stopped to see who he might be, and when he came close, I thought I had seen the stranger somewhere, but could not tell where. And then he began by telling me he had been at that night meeting at the German church, and he had been favorably impressed towards me since that prayer. He had told his wife all about it, and both had been very anxious to know where I lived; they had tried to find out, but had been unsuccessful. They could not speak English, and they had heard that I preached at the English church, and the German Baptists did not want to give them any other information about me than to say, they must not get acquainted with me, for I was dangerous, and the doctrine I held forth was dangerous too. "But the more they spoke against me, the more," he said, "my wife and myself prayed to the Lord that himself would please to make them acquainted with that so called dangerous man. And now at once when I saw you at a distance, it was told me in my heart yonder goes the dangerous man. And I tried to catch up with you, but could not; at last, for fear of losing sight of you, I hailed you, and I am so glad you stopped." " Where do you live?" was my reply. He pointed to his house, then in sight, and said: " There; the old dame is already looking out for us." When we came near she looked wonderingly at me, and her husband said: "This is the man we have been praying for ever since I heard him pray." The old lady reached out both her hands and welcomed me in the house. "Thanks to the Lord," she says, " we will now hear what danger there is in meeting this man." I told them I hoped that the Lord might make me very dangerous to Satan and his kingdom, himself having destroyed the works of the devil, casting out Satan with all his works of darkness out of the kingdom or hearts of his chosen people, and the Lord would go on conquering and to conquer until Satan was finally bruised under our feet.

While I was speaking these two people wept like children, and cried: " Blessed be God who has made you known to us this day; oh how good has the Lord been to us poor people this day." The dinner was

on the table and they forgot to eat it. At two o'clock
I reminded them of it, and told them I must go, my
wife must be very much disappointed, as she had
looked for me at twelve o'clock. The old lady said
she would go with me, and let the old man take his
dinner, as it was on the table. She said she wanted
to know for herself where I lived, as no one would
tell her, etc. She went home with me, and abode
all the afternoon till evening, when her husband
came and also stayed a few hours longer. I found
thus I had found two more believers of my own na-
tionality who could not converse in English. Every
day they came to see us, and conversed on heavenly
things. They were Baptists and had been baptized in
Germany, and had after a long struggle with poverty
managed to save enough money to come to this country, where the man had found sufficient employment
to live comfortably.

Now they desired to unite with our little body, by
letter and experience, but when they had been several times to hear me, they told me they could not
understand a word, and besought me that the same
words might be told them in German. So I concluded to grant their request and preach in their
house every Sunday morning from half past eight
o'clock till half past ten, when our English meeting
commenced. The sweet doctrine of God our Saviour
dropped among us as the rain, it distilled as the dew,

as the small rain upon the tender herb, and as the showers upon the grass! Oh how good is our God. Praise the Lord, O my soul.

CHAPTER VII.

Sometimes I preached as often as three times on one Sunday, and then spent the rest of the day in conversation with some of the brethren at my house. On one occasion, after I had preached once in German and twice in English, we had no company that Sunday afternoon. I felt exhausted and worn out, as I sometimes did after speaking, and my wife went to a neighboring sister to spend an hour or so in her company. When she had gone, all at once it seemed to me that my sins, from childhood, rose, as it were, out of the ground before me. They appeared like mountains on either side. O how distressed for a few moments I became! Involuntarily I sprang to my feet, went to the organ, and played and sang with tears the following stanzas:

> "How long, O Lord, shall I complain
> Like one that seeks his God in vain?
> Canst thou thy face forever hide,
> And I still pray and be denied?
>
> How long shall my poor troubled breast
> Be with these anxious thoughts opprest?
> And Satan, my malicious foe,
> Rejoice to see me sunk so low?

And when I came to the verse :

> How will the powers of darkness boast
> If but one praying soul be lost!
> But I have trusted in thy grace
> And shall again behold thy face."

Then of a sudden an indescribable joy and peace filled my heart with thankfulness and praise.

I saw my sins all drowned in Jesus' blood and I sang the last verse of that beautiful hymn :

> "What'er my fears or foes suggest
> Thou art my hope, my joy, my rest;
> My heart shall feel thy love and raise
> My cheerful voice to songs of praise."

One Sunday morning I went to the house of our German brother (whose name was Hoeflein) and when I just had stepped out of my door, these words came to me with power, and I knew from whence they came: " They shall mourn for him, as one mourneth for his only son, and shall be in bitterness for his first-born." Zech. 12:10. Immediately I saw in spirit the sufferings of the Lord Jesus Christ. Look where I would I saw him scourged, insulted, spit upon; I cannot tell here how it affected me. When I came to the house of the aforesaid brother they saw me in tears. I told them of the wonderful vision, but could not half tell how I had felt under it. The Shepherd smitten with the sword of justice,

which had awakened against Him, that the sheep
might be spared. The Holy One of God treated as
though he were a vagabond, a felon, a transgressor,
that sinful people might be honored and viewed as
justified freely from all things, as though they never
had sinned at all! The King insulted by his subjects, whose sins he bore! The Lamb of God condemned to die, that condemned wretches might enjoy the blessings of eternal life! The Angel of the
Everlasting Covenant put to shame, that all that the
Father had given him should be forever honored,
and crowned with glory, honor and immortality!
O! he hath trodden the winepress alone, and of the
people there was none with him. Thrice he ran
back and forth as though he sought some help of
man! O wondrous sight! To see the Son of God
fall on his face and to see him sweating great drops
of blood, which the sins of his guilty world forced,
as it were, through the pores of his skin! Immanuel, God with us! Men and devils had united in
the hour and power of darkness, to slay Thee, not
knowing that thereby I should escape free from
wrath! "He was oppressed and afflicted, yet he
opened not his mouth: he is brought as a lamb to
the slaughter, and as a sheep before the shearers is
dumb, so he opened not his mouth." Isa. 53:7. This
was mourning and to be in bitterness over sin and
over a suffering Saviour.

On the cold ground, methinks I see
My Saviour kneel and pray for me,
   O let me him adore!
Seiz'd with a chilly sweat throughout,
Blood drops did force their passage out,
   Through every opening pore.

A crown of thorns his temple bore,
His back their cruel lashes tore;
   They made him bear the tree.
In purple robes the Lord they dressed,
Then hailed him King with scorn and jest,
   And mocking bowed the knee.

Thus up the hill he slowly rose,
Surrounded by relentless foes,
   At length his cross they rear:
O can you see the Son of God
 Cry out beneath sin's heavy load
   Without one thankful tear?

Thus bearing our iniquity
He dies in anguish on the tree,
   What tongue his grief can tell?
The shudd'ring rocks their heads recline,
The morning sun refused to shine,
   When the Redeemer fell.

Shout, brethren, shout in songs divine,
He drank the gall to give us wine,
   To quench our parching thirst:
Seraphs, advance your voices higher,
Bride of the Lamb, unite the choir,
   And laud the precious Christ.

Thus in mercy God did show me a little of the

finished work of Christ, and thus he prepared me in
measure for troubles yet to come. I received a letter
or urgent invitation from the Goshen church in Indiana to come over and visit them. I went. There I
met several of our Elders, and also one whose name
was Joseph Smart. This dear brother was loved and
received by only a few of the Old School Baptists.
But as many as received him, they discovered the
power of a child of God in him, and loved him for
the truth's sake. The people delighted to hear him
preach, and in his conversation he was powerful,
and in his prayers he was touching. His walk was
that of a man taught of God, and in doctrine or
teaching he showed uncorruptness, gravity, sincerity.
To me he was a teacher in Israel, a leader, a minister
and a lover of good men—a favorite of my Lord
Jesus and a follower of the Lamb of God. Often
have I wished that his mantle might fall on me.
I desired him to accompany me to Evansville
and to preach for me. He was well received,
but not by all; because he was not in favor of
Associations. Finally the church went out of the
Association. Some were satisfied and others were
not. All this was separating the precious from the
vile, but it brought down the wrath of some Elders
upon Brother Smart. They declared him to be a
wolf in sheep's clothing. I differed from them in
this, forasmuch as I saw in him the image of Jesus.
Now the Elders desired me to have no more to do

with "old man Smart," as they were pleased to call
him. I could not comply. My name too must now
be cast out as evil. The widow Mott and her children went back to New York, and the bitter party
in the church were now more against me than ever.
Finally I withdrew from the church and moved to
Corydon, Indiana, because Brother Smart preached
there very frequently. The brethren of the Goshen
church received me, as a church which had also
withdrawn from the Association, because they (the
Association) had become so carnalized that you could
not distinguish them from the world. We had a
season of peace and brotherly love with all the brethren except the Elders, who would continue to be
busybodies in other men's matters. But I must
bring this sad occurrence to a close. I have always
desired to worship God in spirit, and have no. confidence in the flesh, I must not dwell on the
works of the flesh. The flesh is not taught of God,
and therefore can be content with man-made ministers. They tell us we ought to love one another;
but the question is: *who are* these "one another?"
For if godly love does not act spontaneously without any creature exhorting or commanding, it will
not act at all. When two people are made manifest to one another, immediately an union of spirit
takes place. When they know one another as poor
bankrupts, both prisoners of hope, both poor lep-
ers, both feel that without eternal redemption, justi-
fying righteousness, and electing mercy interposing

for them, they must perish. No language can describe the high estimation in which from their very hearts they hold the truth, yet they can not speak with confidence of interest in the salvation of God, only in proportion as they realize the love of God and salvation of Christ; and this can be only by the anointing of the Holy Spirit. The more they are tempted, tried, humbled, and hunted out of all fleshly hopes, the more are they concerned for an increase of God. As the Lord grants His mercy, and shews His salvation, so are they encouraged still to seek him, and stand by the truth, through evil as well as through good report. These cords of union are forever: all others, even the dearest, must break. I fully agree with an English writer, who calls himself " A Little Brother," when he says : " Brotherly love cannot extend to those who do not appear to be brought out of nature into grace." It is *impossible* to feel towards those who do not love and receive the truth, that which is felt towards those who do know the truth. It is the special love of God, and has its special objects and ends: its objects are God and his people; its ends are the good of the soul and the glory of God. This love is unquenchable—both as it is in God towards the people, and as it is in the people towards God. How many think they have a love to the brethren, but when brought to the test, prove they have not. Brotherly love is not after the flesh, but after the Spirit: and stands in those rela-

tions which are spiritual. Their relations, according
to the foreknowledge of God, is one of the relations
in which the Lord receives his people, and in which
they receive him, and receive one another. And
those who have no union to the brethren in these
relations, give, by their enmity to the truth, more
evidence that they are the seed of the serpent, than
that they are of God : for he that is of God, loveth
the *children* of God. * * What then, does it follow,
that because brotherly love can extend only to the
brethren, that others are to be hated? Verily, no ;
there is a law of *universal* love, as well as the grace
of *special* love. Christ as man was under the law of
universal love ; therefore it is that he manifested
hatred to no man, but went about doing good to all
men—sympathizing with them in their troubles, and
even wept over the city of Jerusalem ; knowing when
he did so, that the things which belonged to their
peace as a nation were now hidden from their eyes,
and He would often have gathered the people together to instruct them for their good ; this the rulers
sought to hinder. But we are not to confound this
general sympathy with men, nor put it in the place
of that special love which he had to his disciples.
The one ended at his death, the other endureth forever. So the children of God are under the law of
universal love ; that is to say, they are not author-
ized to hate any man—mind, I am not saying an-
tipathies do not exist, for, alas ! they do even among

the heirs of a better world. The feeling of the christian when in his right mind is general good will towards men, even his enemies; but this and brotherly love in a spiritual sense are widely different. One arises from the oneness of the human race, being all of one original father and mother; in this sense, all are brethren. But brotherly love in a spiritual sense must arise from being born, not of blood, nor of the will of the flesh, nor of the will of man, but of God. * * It must be by the Holy Ghost, he alone can shed it abroad in the heart."

CHAPTER VIII.

That same year (1869) when it pleased God for me to obtain the fellowship of Brother Smart, I also heard of Elder Burnam, the editor of the "Regular Baptist Magazine." I subscribed for it. He sent me four numbers at once. In one of them I found a letter published in June, 1869. I had written that letter to Elder Joseph Smart, who had sent it to Brother Burnam for publication. The beloved reader may not blame me to have it re-published in this little work. (See Mag., June, 1869, p. 356):

" *Very Dear Brother Joseph Smart:*

It has, for some time, been the desire of my mind to write to you. At times, I have proposed sending you a long letter, believing you to be one of the Lord's tried, tempest-tossed children; and then again, under a sense of my unworthiness, I have thought that few words would-better become me, as I am made to doubt your being benefited by anything that I could write. For truly, of all the saints, I am less than the least, and of sinners the chief; unworthy to be called a minister of Christ, since my heart and my mind, unfilled with the doctrine of redeeming grace, have often strayed after the vain, foolish things of the world, working in me that which is unworthy of my blessed Lord, and hurtful to the soul. But I am made to hope that I did it ignorantly. God did not allow me to continue that way. He set his hand a second and a third time to the work, and brought me to a feeling sense of my need of power and unction from the Holy One. And now I could wish to give you a faint view of what we have heard with our ears, and of which our eyes have seen, and our hands have handled of the Word of life. I know this will do my brother's heart good: for it has graciously pleased the Lord to make you manifest to my poor soul as a father in Israel, as one through whom He has turned many to righteousness. And as I call to mind your labors of love, I would earnestly invoke Israel's God to bless you with the choicest blessings from on high; give you beauty for ashes, the garment of praise for the spirit of heaviness. May the fragrance of the sweet name

8

of Jesus perfume your heart and tongue, and may
you long be enabled at times to sound forth the
praises of our God.

"From day to day I am made to feel more and
more the richness, freedom and sovereignty of God's
grace, finding it in my straits just suited to my
fallen and undone condition. From the ocean, without bottom or shore, flows every stream of mercy
and rill of comfort to the church of the living God,
on their way to the kingdom of glory. From the
treasury and storehouse of divine grace, what a sum
of mercies have proceeded. From thence the first ray
of divine light entered the mind; the first conviction
of guilt stung the conscience; the first sense of condemnation filled the soul with terror; the first desire after reconciliation, the first hope in God's
mercy, and a sense of pardoning love, brought unutterable joy and peace to the quickened soul:

> "Oh to grace how great a debtor,
> Daily I *rejoice* to be."

This grace has been, and is applied to quicken,
to uphold, to support, to lead and comfort every
subject of the entire "election of grace," on their
way to the City, where they shall at length appear
"to the praise of the glory of His grace." I rejoice
to believe that it was by this glorious and reigning
grace that I, even I, a vile, ungodly sinner, was enabled to hear the voice of the Son of God. By this,

Jehovah made me to tremble at His word. Grace
convinced me of my sinful and ruined condition,
and made me a subject of mourning, trembling and
distress. O the sighs and tears and bitter groans,
when first awakened to see my wretched condition!
The pit of despair yawned before me, and the dreadful thought of dwelling with devils seized my mind
while I was made to acknowledge God's justice in
such a doom. Night and day for a long season, sad
complaints and groans were my only companions.
Seeing only my evil and depraved nature, I felt
ashamed, condemned, convicted and guilty. Many
a time I felt tempted to destroy myself, but as often
did grace whisper, " who can tell but what there is
mercy yet;" and so I was rescued out of the mouth
of the lion. Blind and ignorant, I knew not that it
was God the Holy Ghost affording me relief, and
ministering grace to keep me from sinking in despair. At last, I fell a broken vessel at the feet of
Jesus, with a full conviction and desire that if I
must perish, to do so at Jesus' feet; and, O wonder,
grace had-never left me! O sweet moments, never
to be forgotten! I cannot describe the glory I discovered in my blessed, suffering Saviour. Was it
for me He endured such agony upon the cross? for
me His sacred hands and feet were pierced with iron
nails, while from his wounded side the blood that
cleanses from all sin gushed down his holy body on
the tree? Was it for sins of mine he bore the curse,

the wrath and vengeance of God's holy law, while
his very soul, forsaken of God, poured forth in anguish his bitter cry? At such a view, I stood speechless and amazed. I wondered and adored. I was
overwhelmed that such a worm should receive of
his mercy, and yet I could not doubt. Sweet words
of comfort cheered my heart: " Come unto me thou
weary and heavy laden, and I will give thee rest."
Rest for my soul was promised, both for this life
and that which is to come; while joy, peace and
hope were the welcome guests of my heart. I was
filled to overflowing with gratitude, while tears of
love streamed down my face. How can I tell the
beauty I found, the worth and preciousness of Jesus,
the Pearl of great price? Blessed promises were
revealed to me, and sweet views of the plan of salvation, embracing, as it does, sinners of the deepest
dye. How dearly did my poor soul love the King
of Zion, and dread the thought of sinning against
him more! But, O my beloved brother, what can I
say? Twenty and two years have passed since the
time the Lord first appeared to me in pardoning
love, and what am I now? Ah! woe is me! my
vileness and proneness to sin are still the plague of
my heart, and for this I often go mourning and
bowed down, tossed to and fro until the dawning of
the day, or until the Morning Star arises again in
my heart. But adored be the Lamb slain! adored

be God, Father, Son, and Holy Ghost, who, under all my misgivings and unprofitableness in all my slips, stumblings, and falls, still remain the same. He cannot deny Himself. His poor Peters may deny him thrice in one night, but one look from Jesus will make them go and weep bitterly; His poor Davids may transgress, time and again, but the Holy Ghost will expostulate with them, and then their couch will be wet with tears. When His unbelieving Thomases *will* not believe, he speaks, and they cry, "My Lord and my God!" When His sick ones are enabled to touch the hem of his garment, their health is restored. When His blind people cry, "Have mercy upon me," he speaks the word, and mercy flows from his dear heart and eyes. And what shall I say more? I have sinned against the best of brothers seventy times seven times a day, and seven times seventy times a day he has forgiven me. I have been sinking innumerable times, and Jesus has stretched out his hand and rescued me. I have been hungry, and he has fed me; in prison, and he has delivered me; sick, and he has visited me; wounded have I been, yea, my soul has been torn in sunder by the hand of the terrible enemy sin, but Jesus has healed me. I have been an outcast by the highways, but Jesus has sent his angel and brought me to his banqueting house, and spread over me the banner of his love. When weak and wounded, he became my strength, and in mourning, my joy; and when almost sunk in despair, Jesus has entered the vessel, and immediately we were landed on the shores of sovereign grace. Time would fail me to tell of all my distresses, and sorrows, and mournings on account of my sins against my blessed Master, and of the joy it produces when he makes himself manifest to me as he does not unto the world. But you, my brother, are no stranger to these things; therefore I write freely to you, feeling it a privilege to meet a companion on the way, whose exercises are like my own. There is around me much building of wood, hay and stubble, and but few pilgrims to share the field of gospel trial and gospel comfort, proclaiming Jesus the burden of the song. I have often sat in darkness and sorrow, having many ups and downs. I have been pursued upon the mountains, and laid wait for in the valleys. I have sometimes felt as if I were a brother to dragons, and a companion to owls; the old man, and Satan working thereupon, often cause the sad outcry, " O wretched man that I am ;" and in the language of Paul to say, " when I would do good, evil is present." Blessed be God, however, in our worst moments, Satan cannot rob us of this *will* to do that which is good; for we are kept by the power of God unto salvation. Comforting assurance, we have not to keep ourselves, nor yet salvation;

but we are kept for it, and it is kept for us, ready to be revealed in the last day. And now, dear brother, let me ask you to pray for me.

Your fellow-pilgrim, a poor worm on earth,

BERNARD GREENWOOD.

CHAPTER IX.

When I examined the contents of that *Regular Baptist Magazine*, I was so well satisfied with it that I sent for it at once, and wrote to brother Burnam the following:

EVANSVILLE, IND., May 1, 1869.

Dear Brother Burnam :

Please find within three dollars for your excellent work entitled *The Regular. Baptist Monthly Magazine.* Four numbers came to hand at once, and from the first glance at the work, and from it's motto, "Fear God, and give glory to Him," I felt that I had reason to believe that the work is of God. I wish you much success in the great undertaking. You furnish to the way-worn pilgrims to the Celestial City a noble work at so little cost. Many a heaven-born soul, panting after the living God, does at the present day feel the want of something more than the mere letter of truth. And with the poet, I for one, have often said:

"But Oh ! my soul wants more than sign."

The world is full of creature religion, creature piety, and creature goodness, which all must and will be utterly consumed when God's religion, which is the work of Jehovah and not the work of men, is written in the hearts and printed in the minds of any of the lost and undone race of mankind. When the knowledge of the exceeding sinfulness of sin is communicated to any of the fallen race, lo, creature goodness fades away like a leaf, and the goodness or grace of God, which leadeth to repentance, convinces us that it alone can benefit us for time and eternity.

Much preaching is done now-a-days, and many so-called preachers claim to do the work of God. Arminians, Socinians, and Unitarians, by thousands, have flooded the country with damnable heresies. Doctrinalists, also, who preach the truth in the letter of it, doctrinally, practically, and experimentally too, have failed to build up Zion, and have brought, and are bringing barrenness and deadness upon the spiritually hungry, starving and panting children of the Most High ; there not being the one thing needful to accompany the word, viz., *the unction from on High.* May the gracious Lord cause your pages to overflow with the honey and milk of the Promised Land; may

they constantly bring us good news from a far
country; may the dew of heaven rest upon them,
that the little plants may grow! May they be filled
with showers from above, and fountains of the deep,
that the garden of the Lord may flourish in the
beauties and excellences the Husbandman has been
pleased to put upon it! And may you be enabled,
my brother, to draw waters out of the wells of salvation! May you be drawn unto Jesus' feet, and
receive of him and grace for grace! Now remember the chief of sinners, as I subscribe myself, yet
saved by grace.

B. Greenwood.

Brother Burnam answered me in a precious letter,
a letter encouraging me to often write the experience of my heart. In the September number same
year, in answer to his letter to me, I said:

Dear Brother Burnam:

Your precious little letter of May last was duly
received, and I have since been trying to write
something for the "Magazine," but could not. Owing to the limited knowledge I have of the English
language, I generally conclude it is of no use for
me to undertake to write for the benefit of myself or
others. Reading the able essays, letters and edito-
rials of the "Magazine," I find I am incompetent to
contribute anything; and then I lay my pen aside.

But when I am trying to rest in this persuasion, I feel something within me that much resembles the feelings I often experience when I conclude within myself, " I shall never try to preach again," because the word of the Lord was made a reproach unto me, and a derision daily. Then I said, I will not make mention of Him, nor speak any more in His name. But his word was in mine heart as a burning fire shut up in my bones; and I was weary with forbearing, and I could not stay. At present I am on a visit to my spiritual kindred at Corydon and vicinity, and during my stay here at the house of my dear Bro., S. B Luckett and beloved family of the household of faith, I had impressed on my mind to write to you, though I tried to persuade myself of my ignorance, which I did not like to see exposed; yet the thought of writing to you followed me even in my sleep, yet I tried to pay no attention to it, and managed to get something to read, and not having told my feelings to any one, Bro. Luckett came in and asked me if this would not be a good time to write to Elder Burnam. I could not now well resist any longer, and at it I went. Though it is the chief desire of my heart

> " To speak the honor of God's name
> With my last laboring breath,"

Yet I tremble at the thought that a worm like me should be so highly exalted. Sometimes I try hard

to tell my Father's children something of the wonderful works of God; and when I am done, I am
persuaded it was such a ,mass of confusion, that I
cannot see how such preaching can be beneficial to
any one; and then I feel ashamed of myself, and
reason thus: " This shall be the last time. O Lord,
if thou wilt forgive thy poor worm this time, I will
never try it again." And under these feelings I
have shut myself up in my own house. When meeting time arrived, some of the congregation being
assembled, would come to my house and beg, persuade, and compel me to go, saying, " O come on;
what's the matter now? The meeting-house is full
of people; all want to hear you."

Well I could not resist. I cried to God from my
heart, and begged the Lord to be graciously pleased
to make it manifest to me, if indeed He had called
me to speak in his name. " Oh! be pleased to anoint
thy servant with unction from on high that he may
know thy truth." And the congregation looked
like they expected to hear nothing worth,
while myself feeling as though I had no tidings. Gradually life seemed to enter into the
dry bones; the fountain seemed to open; we were
led into the banqueting house; sweet communion
with the lovely Saviour was felt and enjoyed; the
fragrance of Jesus' name perfumed our hearts and
lips. His garment of love He spread over us. It
melted the hardest heart. Our streaming eyes bore

testimony that Jesus our Shepherd sweetly led us
by the still waters of His unfathomable, and everlasting love.   He made us to lie down in green pas-
tures, Himself preparing the table and filling it with
the dainties of his house; breaking the bread of life
to us;   feeding our hungry souls with that imper-
ishable meat, and such as were ready to perish got
a little of that strong drink, called electing love,
which is able to revive their souls.   Some who felt
that they were unworthy to to take God's holy name
in their sin-polluted lips were enabled to sing with
pleasing wonder,

> "How sweet the name of Jesus sounds
> In a believer's ear."

And others who had been wounded in battling
against sin could reverberate the chorus and sing,

> "It soothes his sorrows, heals his wounds,
> And drives away his fears,"

And what shall I say more?   Time would fail me
to speak of the beauties of the Beloved, when He appears in His raiment!   When the eye of faith can
behold Him in His humiliation ! Oh what a sight!
Immanuel, God with us, a poor babe in Bethlehem's
manger !—Jehovah Jesus subject to the dust of His
handiwork ! God manifest in the flesh, groaning in
spirit under the weight and burden of the sin of sinners !   The Son of God as Son of Man bearing our
sins in his own body on the tree.   He who knew

no sin is falling down to the ground, sweating
great drops of blood which the sins of His darling bride forced through His skin! What
eyes that see the sight can be dry? What heart
that is capable of receiving but a glimpse of
this can remain whole? What sinner can live careless and unconcerned, who but once in his life was
led in spirit to Gethsemane? Lost in wonder I
gaze and adore, and desire to gaze till I die! When
Jesus thus makes Himself manifest to His humble
poor, as he does not unto the world, I find it easy
work to preach; just so with prayer. When he
pours upon the spirit of prayer and supplication, we
find it easy work to pray. When He draws us, Oh
how easy for us to run after Him! When he holds
me up, I shall be safe!

"Then I can smile at Satan's rage,
And face a frowning world."

Thus saith the Lord: "I will bring the blind by
a way that they know not; I will lead them in paths
that they have not known. I will make darkness
light before them, and crooked things straight; these
things will I do unto them and not forsake them."
That little word "bring" in the text has often been a
source of comfort to me. It is the Lord who *brings*,
His sheep to his fold as it is written: "Other sheep
I have which I also must *bring*." And again: "Thou
shalt bring them in, and plant them in the moun-

tain of thine inheritance, in the place, O Lord, which
thou hast made for thee to dwell in ; in the sanctuary,
O Lord, which Thy hands have established." When
they are gone out of the way, which had been the
case with all, ("all we like sheep have gone astray,")
behold the good Shepherd brings again that which
was lost, as it is written : "And when He hath found it,
He layeth it on His shoulder rejoicing." And again:
" Thus saith the Lord of hosts, Behold I save my
people from the east country, and from the west
country. And I will *bring* them, and they shall
dwell in the midst of Jerusalem, and they shall be
my people, and I will be their God in truth and in
righteousness." He *brings* them with weeping and
supplication to Zion. " Even them will I bring to
my holy mountain, and make them joyful in my
house of prayer." And again ; God's people are by
nature as proud as others, but the Lord brings down
their high looks, as it is written : " For thou wilt
save the afflicted people, but wilt *bring* down high
looks." And again : " Though thou exalt thyself
as the eagle, and though thou set thy nest among
the stars, thence will I *bring* thee down," saith the
Lord. " And I fell to the ground, and heard a voice
saying unto me, Saul, Saul, why persecutest thou
me?" The Lord works and none can hinder. And
in the salvation of His Church he claims all the
glory. He is the Author and the Finisher of their
faith. " And they shall *all be taught of God*. Every

man therefore that hath heard, and hath learned of
the Father, cometh unto me," saith the Lord. And
when God begins His teaching with any of His sinful children, immediately they are awakened from
the death in sin, and "God, who commanded the
light to shine out of darkness, hath shined in their
hearts;" and for the first time in their lives, they
are made to behold the exceeding sinfulness of sin.
Godly sorrow for sin is given them, which "worketh
repentance that needeth not to be repented of." Now
they feel the burden of sin to be too heavy a weight
to shake off. They may seek to drown these feelings in worldly lusts for a while, but they soon find
that that's of no use; the pleasures and vanities of
the world have no charms for them any more.
What they used to love, they are made to hate and
be afraid of; what used to be their heart's delight,
has become irksome, yea, abominable; they feel the
plague of sin, but cannot tell what is the matter
with them; they know not whence this change
came, as it is written: "The wind bloweth where it
listeth, and thou hearest the sound thereof, but canst
not tell whence it cometh, and whither it goeth: so
is every one that is born of the Spirit." Now they
have a desire to look to God, to come to the Lord,
to give their hearts to God, and to do all in their
power to be reconciled to God. But lo! sin is hedg-
ing them in, and they feel they are shut up and
cannot come forth. They would look to God, but

feel ashamed to lift up their eyes to heaven. Lo, God's all-seeing eye is upon them, discovering even their secret sins. They conclude they are lost to all eternity, and may fancy their souls in hell already; but "if I make my bed in hell, lo thou art there," O God. Their soul is melted because of trouble; they reel to and fro and stagger like drunken men, and are at their wits' end. Then they cry unto the Lord in their trouble, and He *bringeth* them out of their distresses. Read Psalm 107, which tells us that from of old He has thus dealt with His redeemed, whom he hath redeemed from the hand of the enemy. The strong man armed is bound by the Stronger that comes upon him. The Lion of the forest that used to cry out against him, is subdued by the Lion of the tribe of Judah. The wounds the serpent of sin had inflicted on Abraham's seed, were cured by one look upon the Brazen Serpent! Though Satan was stronger than all men, and had deceived the whole world, yet one man, the Man Christ Jesus, the woman's seed, bruised his head. Though the enemy is now united to persecute the followers of the Lamb, yet Christ himself shall tread Satan under their feet shortly, finally and effectually. Though he walketh about like a roaring lion, seeking whom he may devour, yet shall he devour none for whom the Lamb was slain. Though he may deceive many, yet shall he not finally deceive the very elect. "The Lord sheweth

His word unto Jacob, His statutes and His judgments unto Israel. He has not dealt so with any nation, and as for his judgments, they have not known them." Thus saith the Lord, " Fear not : I am the first and the last; I am he that liveth and was dead, and behold I am alive forevermore, amen, and have the keys of hell and of death." And again : " Fear not, little flock; it is your Father's good pleasure to give you the kingdom."

But to return : I intended to give you and your beloved readers a sketch of my experience in the ministry, and if these lines should meet with one, who has been tried in like manner with myself, such an one can sympathize with me, yea can weep with them that weep, and rejoice with them that do rejoice. But I desire to send this letter first to our beloved editor, I shall, the Lord enabling me, give you that experience in our next, provided always that Elder Burnam thinks it to be profitable to the saints of the Most High God.

For the present, farewell.

B. GREENWOOD.

CHAPTER X.

Brother Burman came to see us at Corydon, more and more encouaging Brother Luckett and myself

to continue to write, and though I had to work hard
at my trade it would please the Lord to visit me
graciously sometimes in the night. At one time I
rose up from my bed at night and wrote the following:

Dearly Beloved Brother:

In my last, I told you I would give you a brief
relation of my experience in the ministry. Ever
since I had it impressed on my mind to tell the people what God had done for His chosen, I have felt
myself to be an unprofitable servant in the work.
Sometimes I am inclined to think, that perhaps it
was nothing but presumptuous confidence that moved
me to speak in the name of the Lord; nothing but
pride, prompting me to make people believe, that
the Lord had sent me to preach. At the very
thought, however, my heart sinks fathoms, and
trembling I pray with the Psalmist: "Search me,
O God. and know my heart; try me and know my
thoughts; and see if there is any wicked way in me
and lead me in the way everlasting."—Psalm 139:
23, 24. If the reader wants to know what I am, I
answer: I am the subject of two births,—born of
the flesh and of the Spirit, John 3:. 6; hence natural
and spiritual—1. Cor. 2: 14, 15. By nature, I was
born in Germany, in the country of Arminianism
kingdom of Free-will, parish or township of Human
Efforts. I was raised there too, and from a child

was stuffed full of creature religion. Of course this
was calculated to puff me up considerably, for as a
mere natural man the devil had full access to me.
I was ignorant of the spirituality of the Scriptures,
though I knew the letter of the word. Satan having
transformed himself into an angel of light, and his
ministers also, as the ministers of righteousness (2
Cor. 11: 14, 15), teaching for doctrine the commandments of men (Matt. 15: 9), they promise us liberty,
themselves being the servants of corruption. 2 Peter
2: 19. My parents were born blind, though in nature's darkness they would not believe it; and were
ready at any time to ask: "Are we blind also?" My
teacher was a strict Pharisee, a dead man, though he
had a name to live. The preacher under whose tui-
tion I got the greater part of creature religion, was
a blind guide dressed in the broadcloth of his own
righteousness, a three pointed hat, and other phylac-
teries, (Matt. 23: 5); which distinguished him
from his flock. These were the men who were more
or less engaged to teach that men must begin and
finish the work of religion :—if they did not begin
it, they would be damned, and if they did not finish
it, they would go to hell. They brought in Scripture for their creature-religion, text like these:
"Make yourself a new heart;" "Seek the Lord
while he may be found;" "Whosoever will, let
him come." "If ye be willing and obedient,
ye shall eat of the good of the land ; but if ye refuse

and rebel, ye shall be devoured with the sword:
for the mouth of the Lord hath spoken it;" and
numerous other passages.

Now we were taught that men could perform all
this, and I verily believed I could, and I thought I
had kept these things from my youth up. Matthew
19: 20. In my blind zeal, I went on great lengths
in that religion, and was an enemy to that despised
sect, of which I sometimes got to hear, viz., the Baptists. When I heard some of the " pious people "
declare that they wished these Baptists were exter-
minated, I also was exceedingly mad against them,
(Acts 26: 9,) because they were mean enough to op-
pose the ancient and honorable (Isa. 9: 15,) and the
good people of the kingdom of free-will. Meeting a
minister of the free-will stamp on the street, no difference of what denomination, I was taught to take
off my hat, and make a deep bow, saying, " Good
morning, Dominie." Observing these things they
called true religion, for we must try, said they, to
become as good christians as our leaders, and consequently we cannot miss heaven. Can the blind
lead the blind? and shall they not both fall into the
ditch? Luke 6: 39. Yea, verily, had not sovereign grace interposed and directed me to the Lamb
of God, I should have perished with them that perish in their own corruption. 2 Peter 2: 12. God's
everlasting love towards me was stronger than death,
hell and all the enmity of Satan, together with my

own desperately wicked heart. In the fullness of time God sent forth his Son, made of a woman, made under the law, to redeem them that were under the law. The same God was also graciously pleased to quicken me and to open the eyes of my understanding, and I beheld that I too was under the law. The voice of words of the law, the thunders of Sinai, and the sight of the mountain that burned with fire, was so terrible that I was filled with fear and trembling. Heb. 12: 18—21. The glory of the law, which is spiritual, revealed to me my exceeding sinfulness, discovered my leprosy, brought to view my black condition (Job 30: 30) before God, and my mouth was stopped.—Romans 3: 19. The law cursed me because I was so sinful. I looked to the law for mercy, but there was no mercy in the law. It kills, but cannot make alive. I was condemned, and justly, too. I was guilty before God. Under the burden of guilt and sin, I went bowed down all the day. I would try from time to time to seek a place to weep alone, as long as I well could stay away from my work; my heart was sore with groaning; grief and sorrow for sin caused me to fade away. Many a night have I sought a place to pray in open air, because my prayers and groanings were not heard, as I felt, at home. I have fallen down on my knees and on my face, too, trying to pray, but could not utter a word; and I returned home again as I went, with darkness, blackness and tempest. When my parents heard me returning they would scold, suspecting me to have been from home for some bad purpose perhaps; but what were their rebukes, when compared with the troubles of my soul? In the daytime I cried to God, but he heard not, and in night season, but I got no answer. Psa. 22: 2.

Reader, if you know what godly sorrow for sin is, and that it works repentance that needeth not to be repented of, you can understand me. My life drew nigh unto the grave. I was convinced I had sinned against heaven and in the sight of God, and mercy I could not expect, being ignorant of the way by which mercy could reach my hopeless case.

At last the glorious day of jubilee began to dawn upon me. The Sun of Righteousness was revealed to me, the Son of God manifested in me, the eyes of my understanding being opened I saw Him as he had been slain, my ear heard his voice—my whole soul was filled to overflowing. Beauty I received for ashes, the oil of joy for mourning, and the garment of praise for the spirit of heaviness. Isaiah 61: 3. My sins were cast into the depths of the sea. Mic. 7: 19. I was made to wonder and to adore. I praised God and the Lamb, glorious in holiness, fearful in praises, doing wonders! I was saved! I was made to triumph in Christ! I was a new creature! Old things had passed away; behold all things had become new! I was born again, not of blood, nor of the will of the flesh, nor by the will of man, but of God; born in the Fatherland of Free Grace, Kingdom of Christ, and Church of the First-Born, whose names are written in heaven. Blessed be His holy name forever and ever. Amen.

CHAPTER XI.

Again I wrote to the *Regular Baptist Magazine* the following, as it had come to me at that time:

Lo, I Come!

The words came home to my heart, and I thought at the time that I might be able to put them on paper. But I had to lay my pen aside; I cannot write unless I feel the Spirit of the Lord enabling me. I discovered such a glory in the coming of that blessed personage whose name is Jesus, that I could trace Him from the beginning, or ever He spoke and said, "Let there be light," and behold there was light! Yea, from eternity was He the object of his Father's love, and ever since there were visible things spoken into existence by the word of His power, the echo of these majestic words, "Lo, I come," has gone forth resounding through the heavens, even down to the earth! It was sent home to the hearts of seers, patriarchs and prophets; and they, with pleasing admiration and wonder, lifted up their hearts, hands and voices in proclaiming the glad tidings, and singing the coming of the lovely Saviour, who they beheld, as He was revealed to them by the Holy Spirit, when they were sinking beneath the load of guilt and rebellion. "Lo, I come," was whispered through the chosen hosts of Abraham's seed, and they looked and beheld in Him their Shiloh and their Jehovah, their Redeemer, their Saviour, and their God! "Lo, I come," was sung by heavenly hosts when Jesus was born of the Virgin Mary, and they announced the birth of their heavenly King! The very heavens declared God's glory, and the firmament showed His handiwork; for Jesus had come to save His people from their sins! And He found them in the waste, howling wilderness and in the horrible pit of iniquity, full of murder, hatred, and every evil work. As His bride he found her polluted, weltering in her own blood, clothed in filthy rags; yea, she had become abominably filthy and loathsome. As His sheep, he found them all gone astray; every one had turned to his own way. As the subjects of His kingdom, all had gone into rebellion against him, their heavenly King, and thus he found them a miserable company of traitors, who had willingly joined with the armies of the king of the bottomless pit in making war upon the government of the King of kings!

Sacrifices and offerings for an atonement had been introduced, but God had no pleasure in them. Then said Jesus: "Lo, I come!" I come to save my people from their sins! I come to redeem my bride from all iniquity, and present her holy and without blame before my Father, in love! I come to seek and to save my lost sheep, and I will be a shepherd unto them; and if it cost me my own life, behold I lay down my life for the sheep! I come to deliver my subjects, and if they must be bought back with a price, even my own precious blood, I will give them beauty for ashes, and the oil of gladness for mourning. I will clothe them with the garments of salvation, and cover them with the robe of my own righteousness. I will convert them, heal them, call them, and draw them with loving kindness and tender mercies. "I will write my law in their hearts, and print it in their minds, and they shall be my people, and I will be their God." "Lo, I come," says Jesus; and when He came it was to do his Father's will. He came and finished all he had promised to do. He became poor, was made to be sin, a man of sorrows and acquainted with grief; took the sins of His people upon himself, and thus willingly was made sin for them. Hence he was held accountable in the eye of the law, and must in law answer for the murders of a Manasseh, the adulteries of a David, the cursing and swearing of a Peter, the whoredoms of a Magdalene, and the

9

dreadful abominations of the writer of this; and
the law condemned Him because he was laden with
sin.   His holy person was thus reckoned among the
transgressors, and was made a curse for the people
of his choice!   Oh! love unspeakable! what manner
of love indeed!   Oh! my soul, look upon him!   Thy
sins it was that caused the "One altogether lovely"
to weep, to cry, to agonize in pain, sweating great
drops of blood.   And under all these sufferings He
opened not his mouth, nor said that these sufferings
were not his own.   No, He counted thy sins to be
his own, and his righteousness he made over to thee!
O! great indeed is the mystery of godliness!   Who
can trace the amazing depth of it?   And, moreover,
I was enabled, to some extent at least, to contem-
plate that since the blessed Jesus had spoken His
" Lo, I come," the Holy Spirit had been engaged to
quicken or make alive the objects for whom this
wonderful work of God is accomplished and completely finished: teaching them their guilt, giving
them great peace, opening their understanding to
understand the relationship existing between the
heirs of the Kingdom and their Elder Brother: in-
structing them how it was, and why it was, that
Jesus so loved all that the Father had given him;
informing them that it was because the Father chose
them in Christ before the world was, and that in
the election covenant.   He had declared that He
had beheld no perverseness in Israel nor iniquity in

Jacob, " Yea, I have loved thee with an everlasting love !" Thus the covenant stands : God was in Christ, reconciling the world of His elect, chosen and predestined people to himself. Jesus died and rose again, ascended on high, leading captivity captive ; He has opened the portals of celestial glory to His people, and brings life and immortality to light through the gospel.

" Lo, I come !" The voice that raised the dead is still heard, and the hour is coming, and now is, when the dead shall hear the voice of the Son of God, and they that hear shall live ! He is engaged, as he ever was quickening whomsoever He will, and gives eternal life to his sheep. He still raises up men of like passions with others to proclaim the glad tiding of great joy to all His people, until time shall be no more. Once more the glorious words, " Lo, I come," shall be heard and admired by all the chosen tribes, when He who is now clothed with majesty and honor shall come again in the clouds of heaven with power and great glory to be hailed by all the blood-bought throng. When they shall arise from the dead, flying to his dear bosom, His loved inheritance shall ever be with Him, be like Him, and see Him as he is, to go out no more forever ! O, my God, when shall I see my Saviour's face and in his bosom rest ? Come, Lord Jesus, O come quickly. Amen and Amen.

CHAPTER XII.

Now, in order to show to the Church how I was exercised, or my mind was occupied, when evil men and seducers waxed worse and worse, and done all they could to cast my name out as evil, I give you one more of the expositions written by me to Elder Burnam and published in the *Regular Baptist Magazine*, May and July, 1870:

"DAVID AND HIS COMPANIONS."

The man after God's own heart was inspired to tell those whom the Lord hath set apart for himself, to "stand in awe and sin not; commune with your heart upon your bed and be still." Psa. 4: 3, 4. And again: "My soul shall be satisfied with marrow and fatness, and my mouth shall praise Thee with joyful lips when I remember Thee in the night watches." Psa. 63: 5, 6. Although those precious words were recorded thousands of years before we were born, yet I ask where is the living child of God, even in this cloudy and dark day, that cannot testify to their truth and sweetness? Where is the hungry and thirsty soul, panting after the living God, as the hart pursued upon the mountains, after the water brooks, that cannot tell of some sweet moments spent in communion with the Beloved in the night watches? And oh! precious truth; for every soul that has been made to tremble at God's word, he shall also at the Lord's own time be enabled to rejoice in the Lord with joy unspeakable and full of glory? Every one who knows what it is to walk in darkness, having no light, shall also be brought to enjoy the light of God's countenance, when the " Morning Star shall arise in his heart." Every one who has been made to feel the plague of his own heart, shall also be brought to enjoy the full forgiveness of all his sins, and be made to feast on the milk and honey of the promised land of our spiritual Joseph, flowing with eternal love, everlasting mercies, and grace abounding free, sovereign and reigning grace.

Not one shall be forgotten ; not one shall be overlooked, nor passed by. All that the Father gave to the Lord Jesus Christ " shall " in due time enjoy the blissful smiles of their precious Redeemer! No difference how sinful they may feel themselves to be—foul, leprous, polluted and undone in their own eyes —they shall all know me, saith the Lord, from the least to the greatest. Those that sold Joseph shall see him exalted, as well as Benjamin, who was not guilty of this act. And to know God is eternal life! Jesus says, " I give unto them eternal life." And this " eternal life " is the light of men. In that light alone are they to behold the awful contrast that exists between them and His blessed Majesty, the God of heaven and earth! Sinners of the deepest dye

against the thrice holy God who is a consuming fire!
But give ear, O heavens, and hear, O earth, the doctrine that distils as the dew ! These sinners are not
consumed, because Jesus—the lovely Jesus, the Son
of God, the glorious Mediator between God and men
—intercedes for them, pleads their cause, makes
their infirmities His own, keeps them through all
their vicissitudes of life, and will most assuredly
trample Satan under their feet shortly. A glimpse
of these realities humbles them, and they feel their
unworthiness, whenever they are aware the blessed
Saviour is communing with them ; then they realize that He never slumbers nor sleeps, and verily
there is not a groan, nor a sigh which they may send
up to His blissful throne, but penetrates the ear of
the Lord of Sabaoth ! Are they weeping ? God
shall wipe away all tears from their eyes ! Are they
longing for a clearer revelation of their acceptance
with God ? Behold the Lord will make Himself
manifest to them as He does not unto the world.
Are they made to feel the hardness of their hearts ?
Thus saith the Lord : " I will give them a heart of
flesh." And again, " I will give them a heart to
know me that I am the Lord ; and they shall be my
people, and I will be their God ; for they shall return unto me with their whole heart."   *

Now, I intended when I began this, to give you a
short account of the honey I was made to suck out
the Rock, and the oil of the flinty Rock ; and how

I got a little to drink out of the pure blood of the grape (Deut. 32: 13, 14.) When my well Beloved communed with me upon my bed, when His left hand was under my head and his right hand embraced me. Cant. 2: 6. Ere I was aware His sweet lips whispered, and "the word of the Lord came unto me," and I was led into sweet meditation upon the following words: "And every one that was in distress, and every one that was discontented, gathered themselves unto him, and he became a captain over them." 1 Sam. 22: 2.

The text speaks of David when he fled before Saul and hid himself in the cave of Adullam. The Holy Ghost said by Peter (Acts 2: 20,) "Men and brethren, let me freely speak unto you of the patriarch David, that he is both dead and buried, and his sepulchre is with us unto this day. Therefore, being a prophet, and knowing that God had sworn with an oath to him, that of the fruit of his loins, according to the flesh, he would raise up Christ to sit on his throne." For I was led to believe that this patriarch, this prophet was, at the time the above narrative literally transpired, a fit type of Christ, the spiritual David, the High Priest of our profession, the Captain of our salvation, even Jesus the Lord of lords, and King of kings. And the people that gathered themselves to David are (in my view) a fit type of the Church of God, not only of the Jews, but also of the Gentiles. The text finds David in the cave. This agrees with what the Apostle has declared, saying: "They wandered in deserts, and in mountains, and in dens and caves of the earth." And when his (David's) brethren and all his father's house heard it, they went down thither to him. By some way or other they heard of David's being there. I thought I discovered a great beauty in this typical history. I behold our spiritual David, even Jesus, bowing the heavens and coming down to this earth, and like his dear people, the lovely Being wandered about in deserts, mountains, etc., being destitute, tormented, and afflicted; and that His brethren, and all his father's house, come down to Him in the valley of humiliation, as soon as they " hear " of him, as it is written : " As soon as they hear of me, they shall obey me." Psalms 18 : 44.

David's relatives, according to the flesh, may here signify the elect of the Jewish nation ; of whom, according to the flesh, Christ came. But there were also given to Christ a people that were Gentiles in the flesh, of whom it was said : " That at that time they were without Christ, being aliens from the commonwealth of Israel, and strangers from the covenant of promise, having no hope, and without God in the world." Do not the men that came to David in the cave, somewhat resemble these hopeless outcasts? And these Gentile sinners Jesus meant to bring to his fold. He said: "Other sheep I have which are not of this fold; them also I must bring, and they shall hear my voice, and there shall be one fold and one shepherd." Hence, not only the elect out of the Jews, but also as many as are ordained to eternal life, of the Gentiles, shall obtain that grace which was given them in Christ Jesus before the world began. But these sinners will not come until they hear the voice of the Son of God. They are dead in trespasses and in sins, and must first be quickened. The Holy Spirit is engaged to quicken, or make alive, every heir of glory, both Jews and Gentiles, by the voice of the Son of God. And so Jesus says: "The hour is coming, and now is, when the dead shall hear the voice of the Son of God: and they that hear shall live!"

"His voice as the sound of the dulcimer sweet,
Is heard through the shadows of death."

What was it that brought these distressed, bank-rupt, discontented men to David? They, perhaps, discovered in him their future king, who alone could elevate them from their low condition. But, be this as it may, we know the reason why every one that is in distress, on account of sin, comes to Jesus. The reason is this: "I have loved thee with an everlasting love, therefore with loving kindness have I drawn thee." The Holy Spirit shows them their sins (John 16), and thus they are brought in distress. For thus saith the Lord: "Behold, I will sling out the inhabitants of the land at this once,

and will distress them, that they may find it so."
When the Lord commences His wonderful work in
the heart, then they find that their former pride is
broken in sunder. "Fools because of their trans-
gression, and because of their iniquities, are afflicted;
their soul abhors all manner of meat, and they draw
near unto the gates of death!" They may struggle
awhile, vainly imagining they may obtain rest for
their souls, by something that they can do, but soon
they find that the roll of sins innumerable is spread
before their eyes, and it is written within and without, and there is written therein lamentation, and
mourning, and woe!

What sinner is there on earth that is not brought
into soul-trouble and deep distress, when his sins are
discovered in the light of God's countenance? The
law, being just and holy, continually cries in his
ear: "Transgressor!" "transgressor!" And, go
whither he may, he sees himself a covenant breaker,
a murderer, a sinner, guilty and undone! When
Moses saw the sight, he said: "I exceedingly fear
and quake." But the same God who leads to Sinai,
also brings to Zion! For there shall be a day that
watchmen upon the mount Ephraim shall cry:
"Arise ye, and let us go up to Zion, unto the Lord
our God." And how shall they come? They shall
come with weeping and with supplication; I (the
Lord) will lead them. They cry unto the Lord in
their trouble, and He saveth them out of their dis-

tresses. He sent his word and He healed them, and delivered them from their destruction. Then they praise the Lord for his goodness, and for his wonderful works to the children of men. And let them sacrifice the sacrifices of thanksgiving and declare His works with rejoicing.

Again : Not only some that were in distress came to David in the cave of Adullam, but every one of them. Even so shall not only some that are in soul-trouble and distress on account of the exceeding sinfulness of sin, come to Christ, but every one of them. " All that the Father giveth me shall come to me." All shall be made acquainted with the wormwood and the gall of sin, false doctrine, and letter systems of religion. All are brought to know that everything, (themselves included;) aside from Christ and his everlasting covenant, is worthless, loathsome and abominable. Being taught of God, they shall all learn of the Father, the way, the truth, and life of their salvation ; and thus Jesus becomes manifestly to them and in them the Captain of their salvation. In this army every soldier who is rich is made poor, and the poor are made rich. Here every sin-sick person is made whole, and every whole (in heart) is to be made sick. They that walk in darkness and have no light, shall be made to trust in the Lord, and to stay upon their God; and those that walk in the light of their eyes, are brought down in darkness, and the shadow of death until they realize that

Jesus is All in all to their souls, "the strength of the needy in their distress, a refuge from the storm, a shadow from the heat, when the blast of the terrible ones is as a storm against the wall." Then, indeed, Jesus is the solid comfort when all other comforts fail, and the distressed soul may rest assured that nothing shall separate him from the love of Christ. Rom. 8 : 35.

Secondly : Every one that was in debt. Not some that were in debt, but every one. This leads us to think that all who come to our spiritual David, come from necessity. (1.) Because they are more than ten thousand talents in debt, and have not a farthing to pay. (2) Because they were given to Christ in the everlasting covenant; and, therefore, (3.) the Holy Spirit teaches them feelingly their bankrupt state. The law requires its demands, and says: "Pay me what thou owest!" Alas, they have nought to pay with! Can not they go to work ?

> " Not the labor of my hands
>   Can fulfil the law's demands.
>   Could my zeal no respite know,
>   Could my tears forever flow,
>   All for sin could not atone;
>   Thou must save, and Thou alone."

Now they are driven to their wits' end, unable to pay one farthing of the great debt, and Justice cries : "Cast him into prison : Verily I say unto thee, thou shalt by no means come out thence, till thou hast paid the uttermost farthing." But sing, O heavens! and be joyful, O earth! the law captive shall be delivered! The Lord God Almighty has laid help upon One that is mighty, and almighty to save. A Surety steps forward in the person of God's darling Son! In due time this glorious news reaches the ear of the prisoner, the prison doors fly open, and the prisoner hears the proclamation of heaven's messenger—the "Comforter"—saying: "By the blood of thy covenant I have sent forth thy prisoners out of the pit wherein is no water. Turn you to the stronghold, ye prisoners of hope: even to-day I de-. clare that I will render double unto thee." Zech. 9: 11. And again: "The Lord looseth the prisoners." Psa. 146: 7. A glimpse of Christ, as the surety, is now obtained, and the soul can delight itself in the glorious truth that this blessed Surety, "though he was rich, yet became poor; that we through his poverty might be made rich;" and so "of his fullness have all we received, and grace for grace," and are therefore made to sing—

> "O to grace how great a debtor
> Daily I rejoice to be."

Thus it is that the ransomed of the Lord return to Zion with songs, where they shall obtain joy and gladness, and sorrow and sighing shall flee away. But before they obtain a receipt in full, they must pass through darkness and perplexities, often have wars, experience hunger, thirst, nakedness, famine, shame, contempt, ridicule, brokenness of heart, and contrition of spirit. The crown is not obtained until these and other afflictions are overcome; but their glorious Captain, under whose banner they now have enlisted, goeth before them, to slay and utterly destroy all their enemies within and without. Under his delightful banner it is easy to obtain the victory. Our Captain never lost one battle! Thousands of foes must fall at his side, and tens of thousands he puts to flight! When Moses meets him with his accusations, Jesus shows his hands, and feet, and side, and Moses (the law) accuses no more. When Satan resists, behold the Lord speaks his rebuke, saying: "The Lord rebuke thee, O Satan, even the Lord that has chosen Jerusalem, rebuke thee. Is not this a brand plucked out of the fire?" When our own heart condemns us, lo, "God is greater than our heart, and knoweth all things." He knows his Son and loves him, and all his humble poor redeemed by him. If sin in its various forms shows itself within, making our hearts stoop, lo a good word from our able Advocate with the Father, even Jesus Christ the Righteous, maketh it glad, and the beasts of evil omen all depart for a while. Moreover, the glorious Leader himself inspires his company to fight the good fight of faith, to contend earnestly for the faith once delivered to the saints, teaches them to believe in a finished salvation, causes them to re-

joice in God's electing love towards them, helps
their infirmities to pray without ceasing, to pray
fervently, love the brethren, look to Jesus, trust in
God, rest in the Lord, and to cast down imaginations
and every high thing that exalts itself against the
knowledge of God (eternal life), etc. But when they
leave their Leader out of sight, or he hides his countenance from them, then they are troubled, and guilt,
rebellion, wrath and unbelief prevail; and when
brought to their senses again, they find the necessity
of standing fast in the liberty wherewith Christ
hath made them free, and they are brought to pray:
" Hold thou me up, and I shall be safe."

Thirdly and lastly: All that were discontented
gathered themselves also unto David. What reason
had they to be discontented? The Word is silent
upon this. But poor sinners, even we ourselves
have great reason, indeed, to be discontented with
sin, and self, and all things else that savor not of the
things that be of God. We were once in nature's
darkness, far from God. But " God who is rich in
mercy, for the great love wherewith he loved us,
even when dead in sins, hath quickened us together
with Christ (by grace are ye saved), and hath raised
us up together (both Jews and Gentiles), and hath
made us sit together in heavenly places (or things)
in Christ Jesus." The first discovery of our sinful
condition wrought discontentment in our hearts.
Then we abhorred ourselves and repented in dust

and ashes. We should have despaired of life had
we not been kept by the power of God, and in due
time been made to hear of Jesus who bore our sins
in his own body on the tree. Jesus! O fit name for
the discontented, sin-bitten and law-smitten sinner!

"How sweet the name of Jesus sounds
    In a believer's ear !
  It soothes his sorrows, heals his wounds
    And drives away his fear."

The moment they are brought to give up all hope
of ever being contented in this life, they are made to
hear of a Savior slain ! The moment they are made
to see him—that is, believe in him—they are gathered to him, and he will in no wise cast them out.
Such and such only are the purchase of his blood.
Discontented with sin and self, discontented with all
the world calls good or great, discontented with all
the visible creation, because they feel unworthy to
live upon God's beautiful footstool, they shall be
made to realize that none but Jesus, none but Jesus,
can do helpless and discontented sinners good. And
they are or shall be made to inquire, "To whom
shall we go?" We, discontented and polluted sinners, whom have we in heaven but Thee ? and there
is none on earth that we should desire beside Thee.

Thus they are drawn by the sweet, powerful and
effectual operations of the Holy Spirit to Jesus. All
shall come. All that were here distressed by reason

of sin shall be comforted in due time, and enjoy the presence of Jesus, in whose presence no distress can remain, who is indebted to none, and who causes the discontented to sing aloud for joy! Soon we shall have done with time and time things. May we enter into the city where all that were here discontented shall be satisfied when they awake in his likeness. There the wicked cease from troubling, and the weary are at rest. There shall be nothing there to mar their eternal happiness—no night, no trials, no sin there. And there shall in no wise enter in anything that defileth, neither whatsoever worketh abomination or maketh a lie, but they which are written in the Lamb's book of life!

May God bless you living children of the Most High. I wish you more light and less darkness than I at present have. May you have less hardness of heart and more soul-cheering and heart-ravishing joys than I am capable of feeling just now. I wish you more contrition of spirit, and with it God's approving smiles, than I now possess. And may the God of all grace bless you abundantly, and give you freely all things to enjoy out of his unwasting fullness of love, is my humble prayer for his holy name's sake. Amen!

CHAPTER·XIII.

Now the time was at hand that I was made to feel that I had but few friends, who understood me spir·itually.   One brother, S. B. Lucket and family, also the loved ones at Goshen church and a few more of the same vicinity, still believed in experimental or vital godliness.   But we were soon to be separated. I moved from Corydon to Columbus, Ind., where I lived nearly eight years in worldly prosperity.   But there I found no one like-minded with me.   Several times I have gone to the churches of our faith and order that did receive the Elders who had done Elder Smart and myself so much harm, but when the Elders heard of my going there, they set the brethren against me by whispering "Smartite," or some other evil report in their ears, and I soon per-ceived that they had no fellowship for me.   The tears, and sighs, and groans which their "showing the cold shoulder" caused me, are known only to God.   I now concluded that my little work was done in this vale of tears; I could find no one spiritually minded.   Poor Arminians had nothing for me to live upon, and so I languished and pined away, as it were, in the belly of hell.   Wearisome days and sleepless nights seemed to be appointed for me.   I now lived far from any one that worshipped God in spirit and in truth; finally I came to the conclusion that I was cast out as an unprofitable servant alto-gether. Having lived about six years in the place, I thought I saw plainly that my name was cast out as evil everywhere in this great country ; yet I would not give up earnestly contending for the faith once delivered to the saints ; not in the letter merely by quoting Scripture upon Scripture to prove the letter of the word true, but rather worship God in the spirit, and have no confidence in the flesh. Instead of loving to see my views, their views or any one's views, established and proven by the Holy Scrip-tures, I contended for God's views (if I may ex-press myself thus) the teaching or doctrine of God the Holy Ghost, which always brings me direct to the Lord Jesus and the Lord Jesus to me. A thus saith the Lord the Spirit to the churches, to the prophets and to apostles of the Lamb and to me. The word of the Lord came unto me in the language of the prophets and apostles, When the word of the Lord comes to us, we bow low, and sink to nothing at his feet, and we hear what the Lord God will speak, whether for correction or consolation. But in my feelings I was like the lost sheep in the mountains, strayed from the flock and no encouragement ever to obtain the fellowship of God's poor again. I loathed my worldly prosper-ity, and often groaned aloud in spirit for deliver-ance from it.

When deep sleep had fallen upon us in the night,

my companion would often wake me, and say I had preached in my sleep so loud as to arouse the children (whom we at that time raised though not our own) and herself, and then had burst out at once crying and rejoicing over God's great goodness to his people. Many times she would tell me what I had said: "Complete in Christ! Praise His name! Without spot in Christ! without wrinkle or any such thing! No condemnation! No iniquity! No perverseness! No sin! but rather all holiness, all righteousness, all glory within, all liberty, all salvation to the uttermost!" Oh! how like nothing appeared all the sophistry of carnally minded brethren, the enmity of an ungodly world, and the malice of Satan combined, in comparison to revelations so sublime! How my poor, down-trodden soul has revived under the love visits of the Lord Jesus!

About this time I remembered of having read in one of the London periodicals of a certain pastor named Daniel Allen, then in Sydney, Australia. I wrote to him, telling him of my desire to live somewhere where I could meet with some of God's people, if possible, every Sunday. I did not tell him that I ever tried to speak in public. I have always been but a little minister, if one at all, but at that time I felt like I would leave all the ministry to my more excellent brethren. So I requested Pastor Allen to simply let me know if there was a church of God in his place, where I might be at the feet of God's dear children, and eat and drink the bread and milk of the word of God. He answered as follows:

SYDNEY, January 2d, 1878.

MR. B. GREENWOOD:

My Dear Brother in the Lord:—Love, mercy, and truth to you from the Lord Jesus. Yours of October 3rd, 1877, is now with me, for which I thank you.

I praise the Lord that he should have been pleased of His free mercy to bless to your heart any testimony of mine, which has reached you from time to time by means of the *Gospel Standard.* How blessedly reciprocating is the life of God in the souls of His dear people. How heart answers to heart, eye to eye, ear to ear, and taste to taste in the sensations of grace.   *   *   *

You described your longings for the fellowship of the people of God. Well, that is very characteristic of the sheep. They love to be in company. How pitiable it is to see a sheep alone on the mountains. They mourn in their complaint and pine—

> " Oh! Zion, when I think of thee,
> I wish for pinions of a dove,
> And mourn that I should ever be
> So distant from the place I love,' '

I like the spirit of your letter; and from its tenor do believe that you are one of the Lord's children, chosen and called and faithful. I rejoice to see that you have been led to see the vast difference there is between the doctrine of grace, as held by the mere intelligence of the human mind and the heart-felt experience of them in the soul by the anointing of the Holy Ghost.

I am very far from being disposed to depreciate a sound intellectual knowledge of the great truths of the everlasting gospel entertained by the natural mind. I rather cherish this, in my family and my fellow-countrymen, as far before the horrible errors of Rome and the Arminians. We seek to build true sentiments into the natural intelligence of our dear children in our Sabbath Schools, and by circulating sound books and literature among our neighbors, &c., &c. But the very great mistake and danger is, in taking this good intellectual knowledge of the truth for a saving knowledge of God and his dear Son, by the power of the Holy Spirit in the production of the new birth, by which we desire a new sight and sense of sin—new desire for Jesus, which must sooner or later end in the possession of Him in the heart, the hope of glory. I find by making this distinction clear in the ministry, my dear young friends are saved both from the errors of Rome and Arminianism, and from making a profession of religion upon the ground of a good natural faith in the sound doctrine of the gospel. They absolutely contend, that though the sentiments they hold are the same ones, yet they must be born again, and have a heart-felt experience of these truths before they can know they are saved. Now this is about as far as you can get the natural man to go, and here we must hand them over to divine sovereignty, for justice or mercy, curse or blessing, love or wrath, heaven or hell, just as the Almighty Lord has determined in the deep councils of His own eternal mind. The Lord be merciful to them, if it be His most holy will. Amen. .

Relative to your coming here, seek the Lord: ask for the Holy Spirit to seal some word upon your heart which will indicate the mind of the Lord to you upon this subject. Try and lay your soul open to His " No" as much as His " Yes." Be willing for Him to command you to go or stay.

Then look out well for His shutting and opening power in the events of His providence. See that he close up your way where you are, and open the way here. I know the Lord has His " Oracle" now as of old, where he says: "Go up," or "Go not up." I know His voice by the peculiar power and sweetness of it. I hope you do also.

Should the Lord lead you here, we shall be most happy to receive you, as in the bowels of the Lord Jesus, to love you and seek your real good.

Your trade is one of the very best in our city. Some good cutters get £7 per week, at some of our best houses in our city. Nevertheless, see to it that you come to us by the will of the Lord, or He can prevent you getting £1 per week. Now may the dear Lord bless you, and lead you, and divinely manifest Himself to you. With love to you in the Lord, I remain yours truly in Him,

DANIEL ALLEN, *Pastor.*

When I had read the foregoing letter I cast a wistful eye about me for a whole year or so, but no opening appeared, no yes or no could I obtain, and no assurance that I might even in time be able to leave this country and go to Australia. But there is a land whither we are hasting:

> A land upon whose blissful shore,
> There rests no shadow, falls no stain:
> There those who meet shall part no more,
> And those long parted meet again.

There are, perhaps, a few of God's poor here and there, who have no opportunity to meet often with the household of faith—whose lot it is to dwell in a great measure alone, and who like their parents of old, are ready to exclaim: " By the rivers of Babylon, there we sat down, yea, we wept, when we remembered Zion. We hanged our harps upon the willows in the midst thereof. For there they that carried us away captive required of us a song : and they that wasted us required of us mirth, saying, Sing us one of the songs of Zion. How shall we sing the Lord's song in a strange land ? If I forget thee, O Jerusalem, let my right hand forget her cunning. If I do not remember thee let my tongue cleave to the roof of my mouth : if I prefer not Jerusalem above my chief joy." Psalms 137 : 1—6.

To such I would say : Fear not, little children ; the Lord is ever gracious, ever wise. Himself has engaged to teach you and to lead you about, to instruct you and to keep you as the apple of his eye. Your eyes may often overflow with tears, and you be ready to halt; your heart may seem to almost break with sorrow and grief; your path may lead through gloomy deserts, and cloudy and dark days ; you may be pursued upon the mountains and laid wait for in the valleys. It may seem, sometimes, as though God, even our own God himself were against us in providence. Satan, as a matter of course, is against us, doing all he can, (not all he would,) to hurt our feelings, going about like a roaring lion, seeking whom he may devour. Yea, more! our own hearts condemning us, because we say, do and think so many things that are not of faith, and whatsoever is not of faith is sin. Hence the sad lamentation : " O! wretched man that I am !" These and many more of like trials may be brought to bear upon us. Still, my dear fellow-pilgrims, beloved of God, this is the way God has marked out for you. Walk ye in it. Ere long God will open your eyes, himself will wipe away your tears, and then you will

10

be able to see Jesus, who indeed is engaged first and last in all your trials. This is the way of holiness. Christ has walked that way, and you his followers are to follow him: you have the assurance that he will bring you safe home, through every storm, every obstacle overcome, every foe conquered, every stumbling block removed and yourself washed, sanctified and justified in the name of the Lord Jesus, and by the Spirit of our God. Then (oh! the blissful thought!) you shall come off more than conquerors through Him that loved us. Then we'll cast our souls at Jesus' feet, and crown him Lord of all.

I have before remarked that near a year had rolled around since I received that cordial invitation to come to Australia; and upon my constant inquiry of the God of the whole earth, I could not obtain any other answer than a decided *no*, which circumstances, as they constantly occurred, showed me very plainly. One afternoon (on Sunday) I came home and found an old *Gospel Standard* on the table, which my wife had accidentally (nay, rather providentially,) found in the rubbish swept from the garret of a stable. She could not read the language, and before she would throw it away, she would let me look at it. My eyes fell at once on something about the *Landmark*, published by Elder Gold, Wilson, N. C. Now, said I, I will write to Elder Gold at once, and ask him if, peradventure, he knows of a place in the South where I might be able to make a living at my

trade, and at the same time hear the truth preache
every Sunday. I wrote to Bro. Gold, and obtaine
the following answer:

WILSON, N. C., April 1, 1879.

MR. B. GREENWOOD—

Dear Brother :—Yesterday evening your kind le
ter of inquiry came to hand. I think if placed i
your situation, my feelings would be much lik
yours. No doubt it is quite a sad and trying stra
to be placed in, not to be able to hear so precious
thing as gospel preaching.

I do not think I know of a better opening for or
in your situation than our own town of Wilson.
* * * The Primitive Baptists have a churc
here—a house in the town, preaching every Sunda;
* * * Hoping you may be led to the best plac
for you and others according to the will of God,

I remain,

Affectionately yours,

P. D. GOLD.

Upon receipt of this letter, I bowed my head an
worshipped. I felt in my heart that the Lord ha
appointed me for Wilson. I ran home with the le
ter, told my wife Wilson was the place where tl
finger of God was pointed at for us. I thought abor
Wilson night and day. Kept up a corresponden(
with my now dearly beloved brother Gold, and ke

Him somewhat posted as to what the leadings of my
mind were, and how I progressed in the way of preparing to wind up my business in Columbus, etc. I
became more and more confirmed in my own mind
that it was the will of God. Circumstances soon
proved it. While on the one hand my outstand-
ings came in, thus enabling me to pay off my in-
debtedness, I shut down on the credit system, and so
I soon wound up the whole concern. On Christmas,
1879, I visited Wilson, and was highly pleased with
the place. By the middle of January, 1880, I was
enabled to tell brother Gold that on the 29th day of
that month we were to be, the Lord willing, in Wilson. We arrived on the 28th. The Baptists here
received us and treated us magnanimously. When I
stepped off the cars, on arriving at Wilson with my
family (wife and nephew), these words came with
power and much sweetness into my heart: " I have
set before thee an open door." I remonstrated, and
said: " O Lord, I am not worthy to be thy servant
any longer; and I have told no one but brother
Gold what I was obliged to tell him. Please let me
set at their feet, it shall be such a feast to me." I
then asked brother Gold not to mention me as a
preacher. I felt my nothingness to such a degree,
and coming among such able and wise, great and
learned men as Elders Gold, Hassell, Woodard and
others, I thought I should have a double portion to
listen to them, and bask in the sunshine of their glory.

But it was not to be so for any length of time. The brethren urged me, and declared that if I had any good news from Paradise, to let them have it. Elder Gold, the pastor of Wilson church, was foremost to request me to preach in Wilson, Falls, and Tarboro. Elder S. Hassell then introduced me to White Oak church, Elder William Woodard to several of his charges, and Elder James Woodard to Lawrence's church; and so I soon became acquainted with a great many Baptists, both white and colored. The open door showed itself everywhere. This was heaven on earth to me. To see and to converse with so many that feared God and loved the cause of truth, was overwhelming. Many times I went where. I could be all by myself, and then with tears of gratitude and thanksgiving have I been enabled to give glory to God. "Not unto us, O Lord, not unto us, but to thy name give glory for thy mercy and for thy truth's sake." Psa. 115 : 1.

Six months I had now been living in Wilson, when a little church, called Sandy Grove, sent messengers to me, to come and visit them for once at least. They came some seventeen miles with conveyance to take me and to bring me back home. I went. Then they requested me to come every other month, and finally I had to go every month. Seeing their labor of love that they so cheerfully bestowed upon me, who am less than the least of all saints, I as cheerfully and readily complied with their request.

I became warmly attached to this beloved people, and they honored me with a call to the pastoral care of their little body. Then I gave in my name and membership there, and my desire now is that the dear Lord may always meet with us, as he has done hitherto, for we have been enabled to weep together and to rejoice together; large crowds having witnessed our union, love and fellowship, and some have been enabled to cast their lot in with us by baptism (immersion), and the dear Lord hath added to the church such as shall be saved.

Beloved, my experience is told. Such as I have, I have given to the church. And now I close with a short exhortation. Remember the church is in the wilderness. But the Head of the church is in heaven. Look not to man when you are in soul-trouble, for vain is the help of man. Trust in the Lord forever, for in the Lord Jehovah is everlasting strength. And now may grace, mercy and peace be multiplied to all the chosen race, is my prayer for Jesus' sake. Amen.

THE END.

ACROSTIC.

Beloved! Now I will tell you my German name,
Ere I bid you all God speed.
Read down the first letter of every line.
Enough has been said on this head.
Now may it please God to
Deliver us from all evil for His name's sake.

My experience I have told you,
And give to the church,
Unfinished as it is.
Remember me
In your prayers
To the Lord, for He is
Zion's God, and He will be our guide even until death.

Go on thy way
Rejoicing,
Oh, thou child of God; He will,
E'en down to old age, be with thee,
Never to leave thee nor forsake thee.
Eternal are His mercies, and
Wonderful His name!
Oh, ye that fear Him,
Love and revere Him,
Drink in His love, sound forth His praise evermore. Amen.

www.ingramcontent.com/pod-product-compliance
Lightning Source LLC
Chambersburg PA
CBHW030126030726
47498CB00007B/2569